# EIRA NOVANE

# ASH OF THE FALLEN STAR

To the ones who fall and rise again, with ash on their hands and
fire in their hearts.
This is your story too.

# Chapter 1
# The Dreaming

*Wings of violet flame unraveling. A city far below, its spires catching starlight. Falling through light so bright it burned through bone and memory. A man's voice calling a name that wasn't hers. The shattering of something vast, like heaven breaking apart. Something dying. Something born within the death.*

Caelin woke with a gasp, her body curled tight as a fist against the memory of falling. Sweat cooled on her skin as the dream fragments scattered like ash disturbed by breath. Three nights in a row now. Each time, the same impossible wings blazing against her shoulders, the same terrible plummet through shattering light. Each time, waking just before impact.

Her hands trembled as she pushed herself upright. The narrow bed creaked beneath her, its frame as old and stubborn as everything else in Elowen's Fall. Pale dawn light filtered through the threadbare curtains, casting the small room in shades of dust and forgotten grace.

With practiced movements, she reached behind to touch her shoulder blades, fingers tracing the skin where phantom wings had burned. Nothing there but goose bumps and the knobs of her spine. Of course not. Just the dream again, vivid but imaginary.

"Record it," she murmured to herself, sliding from the bed. Her feet found the cool floorboards as she crossed to the small desk wedged beneath the window. She pulled her journal from the drawer, flipped to a fresh page, and wrote with quick, precise strokes.

*Dream recurrence #7. Falling, burning. Increased sensory detail. Could feel the structure of wings disintegrating. Voice calling clearer now, though name still indistinct. Physical aftermath: elevated heart rate, cold sweat, mild disorientation lasting two to three minutes. No logical source for recurring imagery.*

She studied her neat handwriting, seeking patterns where perhaps none existed. Stress-induced night terrors, most likely. The human mind converted anxiety into symbolism during sleep. Simple, logical. She'd been working longer hours at the restoration site. That would explain the dream's persistence, if not its specific content.

But it didn't explain why, beneath her analytical notations, she'd unconsciously sketched a perfect glyph she'd never seen before, interlocking curves forming something like a wing or flame.

A sharp pain flared beneath her left collarbone as she traced the drawing with her fingertip. She gasped, snatching her hand away. For a fleeting second, she thought she saw a violet light pulse beneath her skin, gone before she could be certain.

Caelin slammed the journal shut and pressed her palm against her chest. The sensation faded, leaving only confusion and a racing heart. Too much imagination. Too little sleep.

The second bell tolled outside, its brass voice deep and resonant. The Bell of Flame, announcing dawn's full arrival. Throughout Elowen's Fall, shutters creaked open, lanterns flickered out. Market stalls unfurled awnings. Stonecutters and bookbinders stepped into the streets. So did the memory-keepers, historians, archivists, and those who cataloged the intangible echoes of the city's past.

In the distance, beyond her window, she could see the silhouette of the Sanctum Pinnacle, its dome shattered like a broken crown against the sky. The headquarters of the Preservation Society cast long shadows over the lower buildings. She would need to report there later today, after her work at the eastern restoration site was complete.

Caelin moved to the washbasin. The water was cool against her face, grounding her in the physical present. She studied her reflection in the small, age-spotted mirror above the basin. Ash gray eyes looked back at her. Clear despite her disturbed sleep. High cheekbones sharpened her angular face, the pallor of her skin a testament to countless hours spent amid the dust of ancient relics. Her hair, the color of moth wings, fell just past her shoulders.

An ordinary face. A restorationist's face, marked by the careful study of fragments. Nothing divine or otherworldly there. She traced her reflection with critical eyes, searching for any sign that might explain her dreams, finding only the familiar lines.

She dressed with efficient movements, sturdy boots worn smooth at the heels, canvas trousers with reinforced knees for crawling through ruins, a practical tunic, and her field coat with its many pockets for tools and findings. Last came her gloves, worn leather with the fingertips cut away for delicate work.

As she drank her morning tea, a sharp, herbal blend with citrus and pine notes, she watched the city come alive through the window. Elowen's Fall spread before her, a sprawling puzzle of ancient stone and newer timber. Scaffolding clung to half-collapsed towers that had stood for centuries, the rubble of the Collapse still evident in the jagged skyline. Glyphs carved into stone cornices and archways glinted in the early light, some still active, pulsing with remembered purpose, others dormant and waiting to be reawakened.

Below, a scribe-sentinel emerged from her building, gray robes marking her as one of the Archives's guardians, leather satchel heavy with sealed documents as she made her way toward the administrative quarter. Across the narrow street, shutters opened with familiar creaks as Master Jorik, the stonecutter, began arranging his tools for another day of careful carving.

Two archivists in their distinctive high-collared gray robes hurried past, arms full of scrolls bound for the Preservation Society's headquarters. One of them glanced up at her window, his gaze lingering a moment too long. Caelin stepped back from the glass. The Society's interest in her work had grown lately, though she couldn't fathom why. She was just a field restorationist, unremarkable except for her precise technique.

***

The city kept time with an ancient pulse, seven bells from dawn to dusk, each one marked by a different tone and resonance. The second bell, with its low, steady warble, summoned the laborers, the scaffolding crews, and the salvagers from their cots. It meant the morning haze was lifting, and the work of remembering would begin.

Caelin finished her tea, gathered her satchel, and stepped out into the corridor of her building. Builders had laid the worn stone long before her birth, long before anyone living could remember. Like most structures in the lower quarter, it had survived the Collapse through luck or forgotten protection glyphs.

"Mornin', Caelin," called a voice from the adjacent doorway. Merra, the letter carrier, emerged from her apartment with her official satchel already slung across her chest. Her smile was as bright as her yellow scarf against the corridor's perpetual dimness.

"Good morning," Caelin replied with a polite nod. Merra was friendly enough, but Caelin maintained a careful distance from her neighbors. It was easier that way. Fewer questions about her work, her dreams, her occasional disappearances into the deeper ruins, and the way she sometimes stared at the stone walls as if they were speaking to her.

"Off to the sanctum again?" Merra fell into step beside her as they descended the narrow staircase. "They say you're making progress with those old wall marks. Brightest mind on the restoration crew, according to my cousin at the Archives."

"Slow progress," Caelin corrected, uncomfortable with the praise. "But yes, we're beginning to understand the pattern sequences. Some of the preservation glyphs might be adaptable to modern buildings."

"Don't suppose any of them tell how to make bread rise faster?" Merra laughed at her own joke. "That'd be a useful old magic. Or one to keep the rain off my route?"

Caelin offered a small smile. "I'll keep an eye out for weather-warders. Though I suspect if they existed, someone would have reactivated them long ago."

They parted ways at the street corner, Merra toward the postal office, Caelin toward the eastern quarter where the restoration efforts focused this season. The streets wound in confusing tangles, some straight and purposeful, others curving at unexpected angles. Locals claimed the city rearranged itself in small ways after dark, a fancy of course, but one that persisted despite a lack of evidence.

As she walked, Caelin observed the city with a restorationist's eye. Cracked paving stones revealed earlier roads buried beneath the layers of civilizations stacked like pages in a closed book. Mural fragments peeked through weathered plaster. A wing here, a face there, their colors dulled by time. Glyphs, carved and partially worn away, waited to be deciphered and reactivated. Everything in Elowen's Fall existed in layers of time and memory.

The morning air smelled of stone dust, cooking fires, and the faint metallic tang that always seemed to hang over the city, like the ghost of something burned long ago. Voices echoed off the narrow walls as shopkeepers raised their shutters and water carriers began their rounds. Overhead, the sky held its usual pearlescent quality, never quite clear, as though viewing the heavens through a veil of finest ash.

She passed Silvermere Square with its ancient fountain, the water carriers filling their jugs from its worn basin. Beyond lay the Archives, its forbidding entrance guarded by scribe-sentinels, and in the distance, the fractured ridge where half the city had been destroyed during the Collapse.

Most scholars attributed the Collapse to natural disaster or political upheaval, pointing to the way half the southern ridge had crumbled in a single catastrophic event centuries ago. But the oldest chronicles, kept locked in the deepest vaults of the Preservation Society, whispered of something far stranger: love that defied the heavens themselves, shattering the balance between divine and mortal realms.

Caelin had heard these whispers, though she'd never dared repeat them. Seraphs were myths, surely. Tales from an age before reason. Yet sometimes, when she touched certain glyphs in the older ruins, she could almost believe...

She shook her head, dismissing the thought. The rational mind found patterns, even in chaos. Her work demanded objectivity, not romantic fancies about forbidden love between mortals and divine beings.

***

The sanctum restoration site occupied what had once been a minor temple in the eastern quarter. Now scaffolding embraced its remaining walls, and a large canopy protected the exposed interior from the weather. As Caelin approached, she could see her colleagues already at work, some carefully clearing debris, others recording measurements and observations.

"Wenriel!" called the site supervisor, Magistrate Auren, as she signed in. His voice echoed against the broken ceiling vaults. "Good timing. We've uncovered a new glyph sequence in the north alcove. Since you have the steadiest hand and the best eye for binding patterns..."

"Of course," she replied, setting down her satchel and retrieving her tools. Brush, chisel, measuring cord, documentation slate. "Have you documented it yet?"

"Preliminary sketch only." Auren's brow furrowed deeply, creasing his weathered face. "And frankly, I've seen nothing like it. The chalk won't adhere to the surface, just slides right off. The impression clay crumbled to dust the moment we pressed it to the stone." He rubbed his fingers together, as if still feeling the disintegrated clay. "Three different documentation methods, three failures. It's as if the glyph is actively resisting being recorded."

His eyes darted toward the alcove, then back to her. "I've been in restoration for twenty-six years, Wenriel. I've documented over four thousand distinct glyphs. Never encountered one that rejected standard recording methods. It's..." he lowered his voice, glancing at the apprentices nearby, "...unsettling. Almost deliberate."

That caught her attention. Reactive glyphs were rare. Most lay dormant until awakened by specific ritual sequences. A reactive one might show greater significance.

"Did you feel anything when you approached it?" she asked.

Auren hesitated, an unusual display from the typically confident magistrate. "A resistance. Like trying to push through an invisible barrier. And a coldness that had nothing to do with the alcove's temperature." He straightened his robes, composing himself. "The senior scribes at the Preservation Society will want a full report. I'm counting on your detailed observation."

A cool shadow hung in the north alcove, redolent with the scent of aged stone. Nearby, two apprentices were carefully removing debris, while the alcove remained sealed off with warning thread. Caelin ducked under it and approached the wall in question.

There, revealed by the recent clearing, was a stunning vertical sequence of glyphs carved into the pale stone. Unlike most wall-writings in the city, these weren't civic records or boundary markers. They formed an intricate pattern that seemed to shimmer when viewed from the corner of the eye. Caelin recognized elements of memory-binding, preservation, and something that might be...oath-marking? She hadn't seen that configuration before.

The glyphs bore the hallmarks of pre-Collapse craftsmanship. The deep, precise cuts spoke of divine tools rather than mortal chisels. Their very existence was a testament to bonds that transcended natural order.

"Beautiful," she murmured, reaching for her brush to clear the fine dust from the deeper grooves. The oath-marking pattern intrigued her. Such rare configurations, where vows with power beyond mortal understanding were once spoken, existed only in the most sacred sites.

As her gloved fingers neared the stone, something unexpected happened. The central glyph, the one that might indicate oath or bond, pulsed with faint violet light.

Caelin froze, the brush hovering. Glyphs didn't react to proximity. They needed activation, ritual, and intention. At minimum, they required contact and often specific sequences of touch or sound to awaken.

She glanced over her shoulder. The apprentices continued their work, showing no reaction. They hadn't seen it.

She extended her hand again. This time, she removed her glove first, allowing her fingertips to trace the air just above the carved surface.

The glyph responded, brightening like an ember breathed upon. Now a soft golden light wound its way through the violet, tracing the complex whorls of the symbol. Something tugged at the edge of her awareness, like a half-forgotten song or a word perched on the tip of her tongue. Heat bloomed beneath her skin in response, a phantom warmth that made her breath catch.

*Remember*, it seemed to whisper, though no sound emerged.

The pain beneath her collarbone flared again, sharper than before. She gasped and stumbled back, one hand pressed against her chest. The glyph dimmed but didn't darken completely, as though her brief attention had awakened something dormant within the stone.

"Caelin? Everything alright?" Magistrate Auren called from across the site.

She straightened, forcing her breathing to steady. "Yes, just a moment of dizziness. I'm fine."

Her voice sounded strange to her own ears. Distant. Auren studied her with narrowed eyes before returning to his conversation with another restorationist. Had she imagined the concern in his gaze, or something else, something like suspicion?

"Interesting reaction pattern," she said aloud to no one in particular, her voice steadier now. She needed to document this, to approach it methodically. No one else seemed to notice anything unusual. Perhaps it was a localized effect, visible only to the person nearest the wall.

Or perhaps she was seeing things that weren't there.

She spent the next hour documenting the glyph sequence, describing its position, context, and apparent purpose. She noted the unusual reaction but framed it in technical language: *Possible photoactive mineral component in the central bind-mark. Responds to proximity and ambient heat from the observer's hand. Requires further testing under controlled conditions.*

***

When the fourth bell rang midday, the Bell of Passage, Caelin gathered her notes and tools. The morning's work left her fingers dusty and her mind buzzing with questions. She needed air and space to think away from the watchful eyes of colleagues who might notice her distraction.

"Taking your meal?" asked one apprentice, a lanky young man with ink-stained hands and earnest eyes. He looked up from the fragment he was brushing.

"Yes," she replied, trying to place him. Jalen, that was it. New to the preservation team, eager to impress. "I'll be back for the afternoon documentation."

"The magistrate mentioned you're the expert on binding sequences," Jalen said, falling into step beside her as she headed for the exit. His enthusiasm was palpable. "I've been studying the eastern corridor markings, and there's something similar there, a repeated pattern with minor variations. I think it might be a protective sequence, but it's unusual."

Caelin paused at the threshold, watching him fumble with his notes. His eagerness reminded her of herself years ago, when she'd first joined the restoration efforts. Before she'd learned that getting too close to people meant fielding questions she couldn't answer. Questions about why she sometimes stared at walls as if they were speaking, why certain glyphs seemed to respond to her touch alone, why she occasionally woke with knowledge of symbols she'd never studied.

A memory surfaced unbidden: Liana, another apprentice from two years past, bright-eyed and curious, like Jalen. They'd worked together on a restoration project in the merchant quarter, sharing theories over evening tea, comparing sketches by candlelight. Until the night Liana had witnessed Caelin activating a preservation glyph with nothing more than a touch. The questions had started. How did you know which sequence to use? Where did you learn that pattern? They grew more insistent when Caelin couldn't provide answers. The friendship had crumbled under the weight of mysteries Caelin couldn't explain.

She noticed something in Jalen's expression she'd missed before, not just enthusiasm, but a deeper curiosity directed at her. A glint of something that might have been recognition or knowledge beyond what he should possess. He carried himself with the eager energy of an apprentice, but his eyes held the watchful steadiness of someone with purpose.

"Send me your notes," she said, not unkindly but with clear dismissal in her tone. "I'll review them when I have time."

Jalen's face fell slightly, that familiar disappointment she'd learned to recognize. "Of course. I just thought, since you're so good at this, maybe we should work together sometime. Compare observations."

The hopeful note in his voice made something twist in her chest. She'd kept colleagues at arm's length for good reason, but sometimes the isolation seemed heavier than the safety it provided. She could see herself in his eager stance, in the way he clutched his notes like treasures. How many nights had she spent alone with her research, wondering what it might be like to share discoveries with someone who wouldn't look at her with growing unease?

"Perhaps," she said, then added more gently, "Your enthusiasm is...refreshing, Jalen. Don't lose it."

His face brightened at the small kindness, and for a moment she almost reconsidered. Almost offered to look at those notes together, to sit in the afternoon light and puzzle through glyph sequences like colleagues should. But then the familiar warmth flared beneath her collarbone, and she remembered the glyph that had responded to her touch that morning, the one that glowed for her alone.

She left him standing there, confusion and disappointment warring on his boyish face. The weight of his unspoken questions followed her through the doorway. She couldn't risk letting anyone too close, not when she didn't understand what was happening to her.

***

Outside, the day had warmed, sunlight cutting through the perpetual haze that hung over the city. Caelin found a quiet spot in the small garden adjacent to the restoration site, a place where crumbling stone benches sat amid wild herbs and flowers that had colonized the ruins. She unwrapped her simple meal of bread, hard cheese, and dried fruit and tried to quiet her racing thoughts.

Troubling dream. Responsive glyph. The strange sense of recognition that had washed over her when the stone lit up beneath her touch. The ghostly warmth and pain along her collarbone. There had to be a logical explanation. Perhaps she'd encountered similar symbols in her research and forgotten. Perhaps she was developing a heightened sensitivity to the residual energies that some scholars claimed permeated the older ruins.

A flash of color caught her eye. There, growing through a crack in the stone pavement, was a small cluster of violets. Their deep purple blooms nodded in the breeze, rooted in solid stone where no soil existed.

Caelin set her meal aside and kneeled to examine them. Violets were common enough in the city's gardens, but not here, not growing directly from stone. And there was something about their particular shade, a deep purple with an almost radiant quality. They seemed almost to breathe in the thin sunlight, pulsing with a life that defied the barren stone that birthed them.

The sight of them sent an unexpected tremor through her. Recognition without context, like catching a half-remembered melody. Her fingers trembled as she reached toward the delicate petals, and for a moment she could almost smell something sweeter than their natural fragrance, something that made her breath catch and her pulse quicken with inexplicable longing.

Without thinking, she reached out to touch one delicate petal. As her finger made contact, the flower seemed to lean in to her touch, and a brief flash, like the glyph but sharper, almost painful, shuddered through her mind.

*I vow by light, and memory unbound...*

The fragment vanished as quickly as it had come, leaving her blinking in the sunlight. The small flowers swayed, as if nothing had happened, though she could have sworn they now faced her more directly, like attentive listeners awaiting the rest of a story.

Caelin withdrew her hand, heart pounding. That hadn't been her voice in the memory. It had been deeper, resonant with emotion she couldn't name. A man's voice, foreign yet familiar, like something heard in childhood and buried beneath years of forgetting.

The voice from her dreams. The one calling a name that wasn't hers.

She looked around quickly, suddenly certain she was being observed. At first, she saw no one, then a flicker of movement near the Archives entrance across the square. A figure in the distinctive high-collared gray robes of the Preservation Society stood watching her. Even at this distance, she could feel the weight of their gaze.

Caelin rose quickly, brushing dust from her knees. She gathered her things, leaving the small violets untouched, though she couldn't resist one last glance at their impossible blooms. As she turned to go, a single violet petal floated through the air and landed on her sleeve. Without thinking, she tucked it into her pocket before returning to work.

***

By the time the seventh bell rang, the Bell of Veilfall, marking dusk's approach, she had filled several documentation slates and avoided returning to the north alcove. Tomorrow would be soon enough to face that mystery. The alcove could wait; her unsettled mind could not.

As she walked home through the dimming streets, Caelin noticed something odd. The carved glyphs embedded in the cornerstones of buildings, dormant unless activated for civic functions, seemed to flicker with faint light as she passed. Each one brightened briefly, like a candle responding to a breath of air, then faded again once she had moved on.

She paused before one intricate cornerstone, watching as the preservation glyph etched into its surface glimmered when she drew near. When she stepped back, it dimmed. Closer again, brighter. Back again, dimmer. The pattern was unmistakable.

"Response to body heat," she murmured to herself, though the evening was cool and her hands were gloved. "Or perhaps static energy from walking." There were rational explanations. There had to be. The alternative that the city itself was responding to her presence was too unsettling to contemplate.

In her apartment, she shed her dusty work clothes and washed the day's grime from her skin. The water's coolness on her collarbone was a stark contrast to the lingering warmth that pulsed beneath. As she reached for her nightshirt, she remembered the violet petal and fished it from her pocket.

But what she pulled out wasn't just a petal. It was an entire violet, its stem intact, its bloom still vibrant. She had picked none of the flowers. Hadn't even considered it.

She stared at the impossible blossom in her palm. How had it found its way into her pocket? The analytical part of her mind suggested it had fallen in somehow, caught in the fabric as she kneeled to examine the flowers. But the growing sense of disquiet suggested otherwise. It felt like a message, though from whom or what, she couldn't guess.

Carefully, she placed the violet on her bedside table, its purple as deep as twilight against the worn wood. Even in the dim light of her single lamp, the flower seemed to hold a subtle glow of its own, a memory of light rather than light itself.

As she prepared for sleep, Caelin stood before the small mirror, examining her reflection in the dim lamplight. Her fingers traced the skin just below her left collarbone, where smooth, unmarked flesh showed no sign of the strange heat and pain she'd felt throughout the day. No mark, no scar, nothing to suggest the burning sensation that occasionally woke her from dreams.

Yet tonight, as her fingertips brushed the spot, she felt it again, warmer now, less painful. For a moment, the skin beneath her fingers glowed with a distinct violet light, forming a pattern not unlike the wing-shaped glyph she'd unconsciously drawn in her journal that morning.

She drew back with a gasp, but when she looked again, her skin appeared normal. Had she imagined it? Was she truly losing her mind?

"Just nerves," she told her reflection firmly. "Just a quirk of circulation. A response to stress and insufficient rest."

But as she slipped beneath the covers and extinguished her lamp, the violet on her bedside table held the light a moment longer than it should have, glowing in the darkness. Nearby, her journal lay closed, concealing the glyph she'd drawn. The same pattern that had, for just a moment, appeared on her skin.

Caelin watched the flower until sleep took her, and the falling dream began again.

*Wings of violet flame unraveling. A city far below. The shattering of something vast.*

*A man calling a name that wasn't hers, but this time, as she fell through shattered light, she almost recognized the voice.*

# CHAPTER 2
# THE AWAKENING

The darkness tore like wet cloth.

Lucan's first breath burned. He gasped, expecting air to fill his lungs the way it should, the way it had before. Instead, the sensation seemed wrong, like drawing fire through his body rather than oxygen, a bitter reminder that breath was now habit, not necessity.

Darkness pressed against his eyes like a physical weight. Stone surrounded him, cold marble beneath his back, smooth walls an arm's span away on either side. The air tasted of dust, thick with the weight of centuries. A tomb. He lay in a tomb, though he had no memory of how he came to be here.

His hands found the stone above him, a bleak marble that sealed him in darkness. He pressed against it, fingers scraping until his knuckles split. The lid cracked first, ancient mortar giving way to desperate strength. The massive slab shifted, then crashed to the stone floor with a thunderous boom that echoed through the forgotten crypt, sending chips of marble skittering across the dust-covered ground.

Lucan waited for his heart to respond to the effort, for blood to warm his limbs, but nothing happened. His chest remained still, silent. The first limitation of his revenant state: no heartbeat, no circulation, no warmth of life.

*Where am I?* The thought came unbidden as he sat upright. His body moved, obeyed his will, but it felt hollow. As if someone had carved out something essential and replaced it with raw need.

He pressed his palm to his ribs, searching for the rhythm that should be there. He found nothing. No heartbeat, no pulse of life, only the terrible absence where life should beat. The certainty hit him like a physical blow, a crushing weight on his chest, the realization that he had died. *I died.* The knowledge settled into his bones with the weight of absolute truth. Yet here he was, sitting upright in what could only be his own tomb, animated by something other than life.

In place of his missing heartbeat, fire ignited beneath his ribs, urgent and insistent, pulling him toward something he couldn't name but desperately needed to find. The soulmark, a divine bond that defied mortality itself. Whatever force had called him back from death's embrace demanded purpose.

He hauled himself from the cracked stone coffin, its marble edges crumbling beneath hands that trembled not from weakness but from the shock of existing again. The crypt stretched around him, forgotten beneath Elowen's Fall, its air thick with the dust of unremembered names. His legs buckled, and he crumpled to the ground, jagged chips of marble digging into his knees. On the third attempt, they held, though they felt more like a memory of legs than flesh itself.

What force had torn him from the nothingness that followed death? No divine hand had reached into the void to reclaim him. He would have known the weight of such mercy. No mortal ritual had spoken him back to being. The answer pulsed beneath his ancient leather jerkin: the soulmark itself, calling across death and time, refusing to let its other half exist alone. A bond forged in defiance of heaven could not be severed by something as small as dying.

Memory came in fragments, each shard drawing invisible blood: starlight woven into hair that spilled through his fingers like silk made of heaven's light; wings of violet flame spreading against a sky that screamed its pain; a name, Elowen, that echoed without context, without face, only the certainty that it meant everything. That without it, he meant nothing.

The soulmark over his heart flared to life, a glyph of ancient origin burning with a golden fire that shone through the leather. The mark pulled him upward with inexorable force, toward something lost, someone forgotten. To someone who must remember, or he would cease to be. He understood with terrible clarity that he existed only because somewhere above, she still drew breath. The second limitation of his revenant state: his existence was tethered to hers.

He climbed the narrow passages with methodical care, testing each foothold before trusting his weight to a stone that had waited centuries in darkness. The passage wound through foundation stones older than memory, through chambers where coffins had crumbled to powder and names had worn to whispers. Water pooled in the deeper places, black and still.

As he passed one such pool, movement on its surface caught his attention. He paused, leaning closer. The reflection that stared back was his own, and not. The face he remembered had carried warmth, color, and the marks of sun and laughter. Winter moonlight carved this visage; its skin was pale as bleached bone. But it was the eyes that made him recoil. The left remained dark as he recalled, but the right bore a ring of pale golden fire around the iris. It burned with a cold light that had no place in mortal flesh.

Lucan touched his face with trembling fingers, watching the reflection mirror the gesture. Real, then. The golden ring pulsed with his attention, and with it came knowledge he had not sought: divine judgment worn in flesh. A mark inflicted for daring to love what mortal hands should never have touched. He had been a guardian once, sworn to protect and observe, never to desire. That oath lay as shattered as the heaven he'd once protected.

His altered eye cut through the darkness with unnatural clarity, revealing details the left eye missed, a remnant of his divine powers, though significantly diminished. Guardian's training, perhaps, adapted to this new existence, the ability to see truth through shadow, to read the stories carved in stone. Each step carried him higher, from worn stone to worked stone, from roughhewn passages to crafted stairs, until at last he found a door that opened into morning.

***

Fourth bell tolled as he emerged, its steady warble echoing across Elowen's Fall. The Bell of Passage. The knowledge came unbidden, certain as the absence of his heartbeat. How many times had this bell rung while he lay in darkness? A thousand years? More? The centuries blurred together like ink in water, formless and vast. He knew only that empires had risen and fallen, that the stars themselves shifted in their courses, and still he had waited in that stone embrace.

The city spread before him in the early light, half ruin and half resurrection, caught between what had been and what might yet become. Scaffolding embraced broken towers like splints on shattered bone. Fresh mortar sealed ancient wounds where patient hands worked to heal the scars of catastrophe.

The living and the lost, tangled together in streets that remembered different shapes.

Though centuries had passed, Lucan recognized the bones of the city. The same mountains framed the eastern horizon; the same river curved along the western edge. Knowledge of its current state came to him through the soulmark, fragments of awareness filtering through their connection, though Elowen herself did not remember. The mark not only bound him to her but also connected him to her present reality.

He stood in the alley mouth, learning to exist again. The morning sun struck his outstretched hand, and for one terrible moment, he could see through his knuckles to the cobblestones below. Translucent as old glass, revealing the third limitation of his revenant form: instability. The vision lasted only a heartbeat, the heartbeat he didn't have, before flesh reasserted itself, solid and pale but there.

Lucan stepped into the street with careful precision. The citizens of Elowen's Fall moved around him like water around stone, not seeing precisely but sensing. A merchant wheeling his cart veered left without looking up. A washerwoman paused midstep, shivered despite the morning warmth, and hurried on. Children's laughter faded as he passed, though no one could say why the air suddenly grew heavier.

Only a few truly saw. An old man sweeping his threshold went pale as parchment, fingers forming a warding sign passed down through generations. A girl carrying water buckets caught sight of his marked eye, that pale ring of golden fire, and dropped her burden. Clay shattered across stone, water spreading in dark pools that reflected nothing.

Most citizens of Elowen's Fall knew only fragments of the divine history, children's tales and superstitions, warnings without context. The city's true past had been preserved by few, guarded by those who maintained the Archives and worked the restorations. Ordinary folk remembered only enough to fear what they didn't understand.

He walked deeper into the city, following the pull that emanated from the soulmark. Each street corner brought subtle variations in the sensation, stronger here, fading there, following a tether through the maze. The resonance intensified near certain places: a restoration site where scaffolding embraced a half-collapsed archive, a workshop where stone dust danced in shafts of light. The work of the Preservation Society was evident in the careful reconstruction of these ancient sites. Their distinctive, blue-marked scaffolding and precisely labeled stone blocks hinted at an organization with significant influence.

Violets bloomed everywhere along his route. Roof tiles sprouted purple petals that had no right to exist. Fountain cracks birthed blooms that defied every law of nature. Between cobblestones, in window boxes full of ash, in the mortar of walls rebuilt from ruin, violets. A trail only he seemed to notice, though he recognized them without recalling why.

***

"Lost somethin', revenant?"

The voice scraped against his consciousness like grave dirt against wood. A memory-dealer hunched in the shadows between market stalls, her cart strung with bottles of captured moments. Dreams swirled in glass vessels. Whispers crystallized in vials no larger than a child's finger. Names floated in jars like preserved moths, wings spread in eternal flight.

*Revenant.*

The word arrived with the weight of undeniable truth. He was neither living nor dead, but something suspended between states, sustained by a force beyond flesh, beyond bone. The living carried warmth, heartbeats, the simple certainty of breath that meant survival. The dead carried peace, completion, the rest that came with finished purpose. He carried neither, only the hollow ache of existing between, tethered to form by threads too stubborn to sever, too fragile to trust.

"I could sell it back to you," she crooned, voice layered with too many stolen echoes. "Whatever death claimed, whatever time eroded. I have memories of memories, echoes of souls long dissolved. Tell me, hollow man, what absence gnaws at your unbeating heart?"

The soulmark flared in warning, gold light pulsing beneath worn leather. She saw too much, knew too much. Revenants were rare enough that most merchants would mistake him for merely being pale and tired. But she recognized the telltale signs, the too-still way he stood, the breath that came from habit rather than need, the eyes that looked through the world instead of at it. The stillness of something that should be at rest but refused to lie down.

Lucan stepped back, recognizing the danger in her too-wide smile, in the way her fingers danced over bottles that held pieces of other people's lives. What she offered was temptation wrapped in glass, the missing pieces that death had claimed, the warmth that had drained from his veins, perhaps even the rhythm of a heart that had stopped beating centuries ago. But she would demand more than coin for her services, and Lucan somehow knew he could not pay.

"Not lost, then," she mused, studying him with eyes that held too many pupils. "Surrendered. Those always cost more to reclaim, the price for what was freely offered is higher than stolen goods." Her gaze fixed on the place where his soulmark shone beneath leather. "Ah, I see. A revenant not sustained by hunger or hate, but by love that refuses to let go. How...inconvenient. For both of you, I'd wager."

Lucan turned away without speaking, but her laughter followed. The encounter shifted something in his awareness. The pull from the soulmark sharpened, focusing from a general ache to a specific direction. His feet found a path without conscious thought.

***

The Old Sanctum rose before him, its dome half-shattered, walls bearing the scorch marks of divine fury. Restoration work wrapped its bones in careful attention, scaffolding arranged with precise care, fresh mortar applied with patient skill. The blue-marked tools and methodically organized workstations revealed the hand of the Preservation Society, whose influence had grown throughout the centuries as they maintained the city's most sacred sites. The pull transformed into an ache that resonated through every hollow space within him.

*She* had been here.

Lucan's fingers found the stone she had touched that morning, though he couldn't know how recently her hands had blessed this surface. Glyph-worked marble, newly cleaned, still humming with the resonance of careful restoration. The specific patterns, spiraling sigils of ancient divine script, were preservation glyphs designed to stabilize and maintain the structural integrity of damaged architecture. The moment his skin met stone, the world erupted.

Violet light. Golden fire. A presence like dawn breaking across mountain peaks, like coming home after centuries of wandering, like recognition so profound it threatened to shatter...

The vision fractured. His hand had gone skeletal, bones visible through flesh turned translucent. He watched skin and muscle re-form with agonizing slowness, each layer fighting to maintain cohesion. His fourth limitation: proximity to her intensified both his connection and his instability. The experience left him reeling.

She walked this city and touched these stones and left traces his bound soul could follow like a drowning man following light to the surface. But she retained no memory of what they had been. If she remembered, if she knew, the soulmark would sing instead of burn. He would be whole instead of hollow. He would have a heartbeat instead of this echoing silence where life should dwell.

A flicker of gray at the market's edge caught his attention. Against the weathered wall, a figure in ash-colored robes stood motionless; he was so still he seemed carved from the stone itself. The hood shadowed any features, but something in that absolute stillness felt achingly familiar. Like looking into dark water and seeing not your reflection but what you might have been.

As the Watcher inclined his head in acknowledgment, Lucan found his own neck bending at precisely the same angle, an unconscious mirror of movement he hadn't intended. The synchronicity sent a chill through his hollow form. For a heartbeat, the soulmark over his chest responded differently, not with the burning pull that guided him to her, but with a resonant hum, like two tuning forks of identical make vibrating in harmony.

His marked eye flared, cutting through the shadows beneath the Watcher's hood where his normal eye saw only darkness. For the briefest moment, Lucan glimpsed not a face but a fractured reflection, features both foreign and impossibly known, as though viewing himself through shattered glass. The vision vanished before he could make sense of it, leaving only the afterimage of eyes that had witnessed the same fall.

The Watcher lifted two fingers to his temple in a subtle gesture that should have been meaningless. Yet Lucan understood with bone-deep certainty that it was an ancient guardian signal meaning observed but not interfered. Knowledge he possessed without remembering how or why.

The Watcher then ceased to be where he had been. Vanished without a trace, leaving only the subtle scent of old sorrow and a palpable sense of loss in the air, a silence heavier than any sound. Not all divine beings had fallen or perished. Some remained as observers, bound by ancient rules to witness but never interfere.

Lucan stood alone in the empty courtyard, his right eye burning with a divine fire that gave no warmth, the soulmark aching with each breath she took somewhere in this labyrinthine city. Yet beneath these sensations lingered a disquieting certainty: in that moment of shared gesture, he had felt not two beings acknowledging each other but something closer to recognition of self.

***

The fifth bell tolled somewhere above, the Bell of Rest, but rest was a luxury reserved for the living.

He had been dead. Now he existed as something inexplicable, sustained by a bond she no longer recalled and a love that shattered heaven itself. The memory-dealer's words echoed: *The price for what was freely surrendered...*

The violets at his feet turned toward him like small purple lanterns, recognizing something in him that matched their impossible existence, life where life shouldn't be, beauty born from stone and sustained by something beyond natural law. He kneeled with careful deliberation, joints protesting the unfamiliar motion. His fingers, still trembling from their recent transparency, brushed one delicate bloom.

It did not wither at his touch. If anything, it seemed to brighten at the contact, petals soft as forgotten dreams against his skin. A minor victory in a war he was already losing.

"I will find you," he said to the flower, to the stone that remembered her touch, to the echo of her presence that lingered like perfume in empty rooms. His voice, raspy and unused for centuries, grated like sandpaper, each word a painful, labored effort. "By whatever thread still binds us, by starlight and sorrow and the mark that burns where my heart should beat, I will find you."

The marked eye pulsed with renewed fire, its golden ring blazing bright enough to cast shadows among the ancient stones. The soulmark burned over his heart like a forge, its heat intense and constant, each pulse a countdown, time scattering like ash through fingers that grew translucent with each passing bell, the air growing heavy with the scent of ozone and decay.

Lucan rose to his feet, determination carved into features that death had rendered both familiar and strange. He was guardian of nothing now, revenant of a fall the world had forgotten, and keeper of a vow that lived only in his hollow bones. He would search through every twisted street, every forgotten corner of this broken city. Lucan would find her before his form unraveled completely, before the borrowed time that sustained him ran out.

A whisper of violet light flickered at the edge of his vision. There, in the shadow of a crumbling archway, a figure in a restorationist's coat bent over a fragment of carved stone. Hair, the color of a moth's wing, caught the afternoon light, and something in the careful way those fingers traced the ancient glyphs made his knees give way.

Then she straightened, brushing dust from the worn canvas of her Preservation Society uniform, and he saw her profile. The high cheekbones, the pale skin marked by years among stone and memory, the focused concentration that had once cataloged the dreams of empires. Different now, mortal, weathered by time and forgetting, but unmistakably her.

The world stopped. The soulmark erupted in savage, burning recognition.

For the first time since the resurrection, his lungs expanded with something akin to breathing: deep, desperate, and necessary. The translucent edges of his form solidified, pale skin flushing with the warmth he'd thought lost forever. His eye blazed in warning.

"Caelin!" someone called from the restoration site. A young man with ink-stained hands waved from the scaffolding. "The binding sequence you requested, I think I've found the pattern!"

She raised a hand in acknowledgment, her voice carrying across the courtyard with quiet authority. "Document everything, Jalen. We'll examine it tomorrow."

Caelin. The name settled into his consciousness like a key finding its lock. Not Elowen. Human tongues no longer uttered those sacred syllables. But this mortal name, chosen or given, wrapped around the essence he knew as surely as his own reflection.

She gathered her tools with the same methodical care she had once shown when cataloging celestial memories, each movement precise and weighted with purpose. The soulmark beneath his ribs pulsed with every gesture, confirming what his marked eye had already revealed. She was here.

She turned to leave, walking deeper into the restoration site without once glancing in his direction. The violet light that had drawn his attention flickered and faded as the distance stretched between them, but the burning recognition in his bond only intensified.

*Elowen. Caelin.* Whatever name she carried now, whatever shape mortality had given to her divine essence, the bond that had dragged him back from death's embrace sang with certainty. Lucan had found her.

Now he had to make her remember, before his revenant form failed completely and the chance for both their redemptions was lost forever.

# Chapter 3

# The Restoration

The glyph screamed.

Caelin jerked her hand back as violet light erupted from the memory-preservation stone, blazing so fiercely that the other workers looked up in alarm. They only saw her stumbling backward, flexing her fingers. They couldn't see the afterimage of wings burning across the stone's surface or hear the echo of her own voice speaking words in a language that predated the city's founding.

"Caelin!" Jalen Mor dropped his restoration brush. His sandy hair stuck up at odd angles where he'd been running nervous fingers through it. "What happened to the preservation matrix?"

She stared at her hand. The stone had felt like molten gold, yet her skin showed only a faint tingling warmth. The glyph had settled back to dormant gray marble, but the sensation lingered, divine fire racing through her veins, wings spreading wide enough to embrace the sky.

"The resonance destabilized," she managed, her voice steadier than her racing heartbeat. "Nothing unusual."

A lie. The fourth anomaly this morning.

Around them, the Old Sanctum stretched its broken bones toward the afternoon sky. Canvas stretched across scaffolding protected the restoration site from the weather, while dust motes danced in shafts of light that filtered through gaps in the covering.

Jalen approached, curiosity and concern clear in his expression. His ink-stained fingers clutched his ever-present notebook, filled with cramped but precise handwriting. Unlike the other preservationists who maintained a careful distance from their colleagues, Jalen sought a connection, a trait that made Caelin both drawn to and wary of him.

"That's the fourth anomaly today," he said, mirroring her thoughts. "First, the binding-ward activated without a trigger. Then the altar fragments shifted configuration. The memory-crystal in sector seven started resonating on its own. And now this stone reacts when you merely approach it." He looked up from his notes, blue eyes bright. "Master Thorin specifically mentioned your unusual success rate with activations."

The subtle emphasis on *your* sent a chill down her spine. The senior preservationists had been watching her progress. For what purpose?

Caelin focused on cleaning her tools, the familiar routine helping steady her pulse. "Practice sharpens intuition."

"The memory-stone you just contacted," Jalen pressed, pen hovering over a fresh page. "What did it show you?"

The truth balanced on her tongue: wings of violet flame spreading against a sky that screamed its pain, a city burning beneath the weight of falling divinity, her own voice speaking vows that tasted of starlight and sacred rebellion. But something held her back, a warning that whispered caution.

"Disjointed images," she said instead. "Blinding light. The sensation of falling."

"Fragments of falling," Jalen murmured, writing quickly. "Memory-stones capture moments charged with powerful emotions. If this matrix contains impressions of falling, it might have been present during the Collapse itself."

The word sent a familiar chill down her spine. The Collapse, the catastrophe that had shattered the Sanctum Pinnacle, fractured half the city, and given Elowen's Fall its name. Official histories spoke of divine judgment or seismic upheaval, accounts sanitized by the Order of Preservation and their careful curation of the past.

"What do the personal accounts say about the Collapse?" she asked, settling cross-legged beside the problematic memory-stone. The thrumming had faded to a gentle pulse, but beneath her collarbone, heat bloomed without explanation.

Jalen's eyes brightened. He pulled a carefully wrapped scroll from his satchel. "This is a scribe's journal recovered from the eastern ruins. Listen to his entry from the night before the Collapse."

His finger traced faded brown ink: "'The stars sing with unfamiliar voices tonight. Sister Morwen came to my chambers in distress, claiming the preservation glyphs throughout her wing pulse with independent light. Even the Archives Guards speak in hushed tones of shared dreams, wings wreathed in divine fire, voices that speak names in tongues that predate mortal speech. The very stones seem to hold their breath, waiting for some word that will reshape the world itself.'"

The description hit Caelin like a physical blow. Wings wreathed in divine fire. Names spoken in tongues that predated mortal speech. Her fingers went instinctively to her collar, where heat flared to uncomfortable intensity.

"What happened the next morning?" she asked, surprised by the hoarseness of her own voice.

"The Collapse began at dawn," Jalen said, consulting another scroll. "But the truly fascinating part is the pattern. The destruction radiates from the Sanctum Pinnacle in geometric spirals, like reality itself cracked along lines of sacred significance. The Archives Ward, where the Order maintains its headquarters, remained almost untouched despite being mere yards from total devastation."

A shadow fell across the afternoon light. Caelin looked up to see a tall figure silhouetted in the restoration site's entrance, lean build wrapped in weathered leather that spoke of long travels through forgotten places. Her breath caught as an inferno flared beneath her collarbone, sudden and fierce as a branding iron.

The stranger's head turned in her direction, and she glimpsed strong features etched in profile. Dark hair, a jaw that suggested both determination and gentleness, and something in his bearing that spoke of watchful patience. One eye seemed to catch the light, glinting with an unnatural sheen. Then he moved on, disappearing beyond the canvas barriers, leaving her gasping with a loss she couldn't explain.

"Caelin?" Jalen's voice reached her from what felt like a great distance. "You've gone chalk white."

Before she knew it, she was on her feet, drawn toward the entrance where the stranger had stood moments ago. The room now seemed devoid of a crucial energy she hadn't noticed until it disappeared.

"Did you see him?" she asked, then regretted the question.

"See who?" Jalen glanced around the site, noting only the handful of other preservationists bent over their careful work.

*Soulmark.* The word surfaced without context, carrying absolute conviction despite her complete ignorance of its meaning. The place on her shoulder, just beneath her collarbone, that responded to the proximity of someone whose significance transcended rational explanation, was a soulmark.

"Nothing," she said weakly, settling back down. But her concentration was scattered. Every footstep beyond the barriers might belong to the stranger who had made her soulmark blaze to life.

"The memory-stones," she blurted out. "Have any of them ever displayed images of particular individuals instead of just events?"

"Some of the more complex matrices hold portrait impressions." Jalen studied her with growing concern. "Are you hoping to identify someone from your visions?"

Before she could lose her nerve, Caelin reached for the stone that had screamed at her touch. This time, she pressed both palms flat against its surface and opened herself to whatever it contained.

Light exploded behind her eyelids, starlight woven into patterns that bypassed rational thought to speak directly to the soul. And moving through that celestial radiance, a man whose face triggered recognition so profound it hurt.

Dark eyes that shone with a devotion beyond mere duty. Hands that moved with practiced precision. He reached toward her with desperate hope, and every fiber of her being strained to reach back...

"Caelin!" Jalen's sharp call shattered the vision.

She opened eyes she didn't remember closing, finding him crouched beside her with obvious alarm. The stone beneath her palms had gone dark, but the scent of ozone lingered like the aftermath of lightning.

"You weren't responding," he said, voice tight with worry. "And you have a mark..." He gestured toward her chest, confusion replacing concern. "Something was glowing beneath your shirt. Bright enough to see through the fabric."

Caelin's hands flew to the spot, finding only the familiar contours of bone and flesh. But warmth pulsed there in rhythm with her heartbeat, creating a cadence that felt more ancient than her own life.

"Strange optical effect," she said, standing shakily. "Older matrices sometimes cause light distortions."

Jalen collected his scattered notes, yet his gaze stayed locked on her face. "The visions you're having, they might not be random images. Memory-stones capture reality, not imagination. If you're witnessing distinct people and moments..."

"Then what?" she asked, sharper than intended.

"Then perhaps they're trying to tell you something important." His voice carried quiet conviction, but something in his eyes suggested he might not be speaking solely for her benefit. "Perhaps you're meant to remember things you've forgotten."

The phrase lodged in her consciousness like a barbed hook. Forgotten things. But what could she have forgotten that mattered? She'd lived in Elowen's Fall her entire life, hadn't she?

She grappled to recall specific memories, childhood friends, family ties, and the usual tapestry of experiences that shape a life. These details eluded her grasp, vanishing like mist under the warmth of sunlight.

"The fifth bell will ring soon," Caelin whispered, gathering her tools with hands that trembled. "I should complete today's documentation."

Jalen nodded, but his eyes held the intensity of someone who'd glimpsed the edge of a mystery worth pursuing. "If you need someone to witness your experiences, to help document what's happening..." He held up his notebook. "I'm skilled at recording details. And I don't frighten easily."

The offer touched something deep in her core, simple human warmth amid her increasing isolation. When had someone last offered to stand beside her in uncertainty?

"Thank you," she said, her meaning far richer than such simple words allowed.

As the afternoon progressed, Caelin immersed herself in routine while maintaining awareness of the entrance, listening for any footsteps that might signal the stranger's return. She couldn't shake the feeling of being watched, not just by Jalen, whose gaze occasionally lingered too long on her work, but by someone unseen.

Once, she caught him making notes when he thought she wasn't looking, his expression troubled. When she approached, he closed his notebook too quickly.

***

The fifth bell tolled across the city with its clear, measured tone, signaling the end of the workday. She gathered her tools and departed into the courtyard, inhaling deeply as the air filled with the earthy scent of stone dust mixed with herbs from a nearby garden.

A flash of impossible color stopped her midstride.

Growing from a hairline crack in the ancient marble paving was a cluster of violets. Their deep purple blooms seemed to glow with their own inner light, petals soft as silk against the harsh stone that should have offered no purchase for roots.

Caelin crouched to examine them. Without thinking, she reached out to touch one perfect petal.

The world exploded into memory. *I vow by light, and memory unbound, to choose love over law, devotion over duty. Let heaven itself break before this bond does, and let the earth remember what the sky forgets.*

The vision shattered, leaving her gasping on the courtyard stones with the flavor of vanished starlight heavy on her tongue. The violet under her fingers pulsed with impossible vitality, alive with purpose she couldn't fathom.

Behind her, footsteps approached. She turned to find Jalen staring not at her face but at the empty air above her shoulders, his notebook forgotten in his slack grip.

"Caelin," he whispered, voice tight with awe and growing fear. "You have wings."

She felt them then, a weight and lightness simultaneously, spreading from her shoulder blades. Not physical, not yet, but undeniably present. The weight of forgotten divinity settling back into place.

In the distance, a bell tolled. Not the measured rhythm of the city's timekeeping, but a sharp warning sound that echoed from the direction of the Order's headquarters.

Jalen's expression shifted from wonder to alarm. He glanced toward the sound, then back at her, conflict evident in his features.

"They're coming," he said simply.

# Chapter 4
# The Flame's Echo

Second bell echoed across the city as Lucan paused at a crumbling intersection, disoriented. The map in his fading memory no longer matched the twisting streets before him. His right eye burned, the golden fire within it intensifying as he searched for a path forward.

An elderly woman selling dried herbs from a small cart watched him with unusual calm as others hurried past, averting their eyes from his otherworldly appearance. Unlike the fearful glances of others, her gaze held recognition.

"You look lost, stranger," she said, her voice weathered but kind. "And carrying a burden heavier than most."

Lucan approached cautiously. "I'm searching for someone."

"Aren't we all?" She selected a sprig of something silvery from her cart. "But your search has more urgency than most. The mark you bear speaks of bonds stretched thin."

His hand instinctively moved to his chest, where the soul-mark burned beneath his leather. The woman's eyes followed the movement, understanding dawning in her expression.

"How do you know of such things?" he asked.

She handed him the herb sprig. "Take this to Mother Evienne at the Broken Hearth where the eastern quarter meets the marshland. Follow where the cobblestones give way to soft earth, where willows weep into still waters." She leaned closer. "She reads what's written in flame and bone. If anyone can help one such as you, it's her."

"Why would she help me?" Lucan asked, accepting the herb that seemed to pulse with subtle warmth between his fingers.

The herb seller's smile held secrets. "Because she's been waiting. The signs have been in the emberlight for days now, a guardian returned, a divine mark burning against mortality." She gestured eastward. "The path will reveal itself to one who carries such fire in his eye."

As Lucan turned to leave, she added softly, "When you find the Hearth, tell her that Yaris sent you with thrice-blessed marshroot. She'll understand what it means."

The herb in his hand seemed to pull him eastward, its scent growing stronger when he moved in the right direction. Following this subtle guidance, Lucan made his way toward the marshy eastern quarter, where stone gradually yielded to timber and moss crept up walls in patterns resembling ancient script.

His form grew less substantial with each step. When he leaned against a weathered post, his hand passed through the wood for a terrifying moment before his flesh reasserted itself. The emptiness where his heartbeat should thunder had become a void, pulling at what kept him whole.

"She exists," he whispered, pressing a palm to the spot where the soulmark burned beneath ancient leather. The mark functioned differently than those of the living, not just a symbol but a tether anchoring him to the mortal realm. "Somewhere in this broken city, she breathes, and that breathing keeps me bound to form."

His time was limited. Each day, the unraveling progressed further. Soon, not even their connection would be enough.

The streets widened as moisture thickened the air. Willows drooped silver branches into still waters that reflected more than the sky. Here, where the city dissolved into wetland, architecture followed different principles. Foundations sank deep into rich earth. Walls curved to accommodate root systems. Even the cobblestones seemed to grow rather than lie flat.

***

The Broken Hearth appeared between one step and the next, as though the marsh mists had hidden it until he proved worthy. Low and sprawling, built of soot-stained wood and stones, settled deep into soft earth. It seemed less like a building than something grown from the wetland. Smoke drifted from multiple chimneys, carrying scents that made his flame-rimmed eye water: dried herbs, ancient bone, and captured dreams.

The door opened before he could knock.

"The marked one arrives at last."

Mother Evienne stood in the threshold, small beneath layers of ash-colored wool, her presence somehow filling the doorway despite her diminutive stature. Her blindfold, woven with silver threads, caught the light like trapped celestial fire. In her weathered hands, she held a bone staff carved from what appeared to be a seraph's wing bone, a relic that would have the Order of Preservation scrambling to confiscate it.

"Yaris sent me to you. I'm looking for..." he began.

"I know what you seek." She moved aside, beckoning him into a welcoming warmth that felt like the end of a centuries-long journey. "I know what you've lost. More importantly, child of two deaths, I know what you're becoming."

The interior defied the humble exterior's promise. The main room stretched wide, its ceiling supported by living pillars where trees had been convinced to grow straight, their bark inscribed with sigils that emanated patient light. Emberlight danced in carved niches; not ordinary flames, but illumination that breathed with awareness and cast shadows that moved independently.

Shelves lined every surface, holding treasures and oddities. Jars of preserved herbs. Bones bearing delicate divine script. Glass vials filled with crystallized tears or liquid moonbeams. Fragments of armor scored with a sacred text that violence had scarred.

Sacred charms hung from rafters on copper chains, turning slowly in currents that carried whispers in dead languages. A blackened glyph-stone hummed with dormant power. Pressed flowers kept their color despite obvious age. Scrolls sealed with wax that gleamed like fresh blood.

"Sit," Evienne commanded, settling onto a cushion beside the central hearth where emberlight burned brightest. The flames reached toward her like eager children. "Let me see what judgment marks your flesh."

Lucan remained standing, hand moving to where his sword should hang, finding only empty air. "I don't understand what's happening to me." His right hand flickered briefly, transparency revealing bone beneath translucent skin.

"Understanding is luxury." She pointed to the cushion with her staff, its spiraling patterns shifting when viewed directly. "Survival is a necessity. Sit before you fade entirely."

He lowered himself carefully, joints protesting with the creaking of something not quite alive. The emberlight settled around him, warm touches that caused his marked eye to throb.

"Divine fire caged in mortal flesh," Evienne observed. "A ring of judgment placed not in cruelty but in consequence."

She leaned forward. "Tell me, revenant. Do you remember the weight of wings?"

The question struck him like a physical blow. For a devastating moment, he perceived them, vast pinions of violet flame spreading from his shoulders, carrying the terrible weight of sacred duty. But the memory scattered like ash.

"No wings," he managed. "Just falling through light that burned."

"Not your wings," Evienne said with infinite patience. "Hers. You remember when they burned away, don't you? The radiance that poured from her as divinity tore from mortal flesh?"

His throat tightened around words that tasted of smoke and regret. The pull in his chest became agony, raw and desperate. "I remember reaching. Trying to catch something too bright to hold."

"And failing." She cast herbs into the emberlight, shifting the flames from gold to the exact shade of violet he glimpsed in dreams. "What do you know of soulmarks, walking dead man?"

Lucan's hand moved to his chest, where heat pulsed beneath the leather. "Mine burns when I think of things I can't quite remember, things that feel more real than this half-life."

"Location speaks to purpose," Evienne said, her staff tapping against stone with the rhythm of a funeral drum. "Yours rests where the heart beats, seat of protection, the guardian's oath written in flesh and flame. Hers marks where truth is spoken, where vows are sealed by breath and celestial fire."

"Hers?" The word emerged as a prayer.

"She carries the twin to yours, branded into flesh that no longer remembers its divine nature. Every truth she speaks makes it flare. Every question about what she's forgotten causes it to burn."

The emberlight surged, and suddenly Lucan saw not with his eyes but with deeper perception. A vision appeared: a young woman bent over restoration tools. Ash gray eyes focused on glyphs responding to her touch with eager luminescence. Her hand rising to trace something beneath her collarbone, confusion and recognition warring in her expression.

*She is here*, he thought, the words carrying prayer and desperation.

"She exists, she breathes, she dreams of falling through radiance that tastes like forbidden love," Evienne confirmed. "But she doesn't remember you, guardian. Doesn't remember herself or the choice that shattered the heavens. Her memory binds your form. Her uncertainty is your unraveling."

His hand flickered like a candle in the wind. For a terrifying moment, he saw through his knuckles to the cushion beneath, bones and sinew rendered translucent as old glass, revealing the truth of what he'd become. The sight lasted only heartbeats before flesh reasserted itself.

"How long do I have?" The question emerged as barely a whisper.

"That depends on the strength of your bond." Evienne cast crystallized tears into the flames, which blazed up, showing fragmented images: a man in guardian's armor kneeling beside a pool of light. The same man reaching toward luminous wings crumbling at his touch. Radiance pouring from a wound sustained only by desperate love.

"You died," Evienne stated simply. "When she fell, when divinity and mortality collided, you died trying to catch what couldn't be caught. Your body broke under the weight of falling godhood."

The revelation settled into him like a missing piece returning. "Then what am I?"

"Borrowed time given form," she explained. "Sustained by a bond grown dangerously weak. The soulmark is more than symbol, it's an anchor, tethering what remains of your essence to this realm."

She continued, "She questions everything now, her dreams, her reactions to things that should be familiar, the glyphs that respond to her touch. But she doesn't remember choosing you."

The words cut deeper than any blade, finding places in his spirit that still bled. "Can she remember?"

"Divine erasure is thorough, but choice remains." Evienne leaned forward. "The law did not forge your mark. Love freely given sealed it. That spark remains, even when everything else burns away."

She reached across the space between them, one weathered hand covering his translucent knuckles. The touch burned with the memory of warmth in living blood.

"Beware," she warned, voice dropping lower. "There is one who would see all bonds severed, all memories dissolved. One who believes love corrupts and choice breeds chaos. They circle her awareness even now, offering mercy through forgetting."

The temperature plummeted. Frost formed on windows despite the hearth's warmth. Lucan's marked eye flared in response to some presence pressing against the hearth's boundaries, testing Evienne's wards.

"Who?" he asked.

"Names have power. This one's name doubly so." Evienne withdrew her hand. "Know only this: they once stood beside her in perfect balance, before love taught her that some things matter more than harmony. Their grief drives them now...grief that wears mercy's mask."

The emberlight flickered wildly. For a moment, Lucan glimpsed a tall figure in robes of dusk and silver, face too bright to perceive directly. Glyphs crawled across their skin like living law, constantly rewriting themselves. Their presence carried absolute authority, recognizing no equal.

"The Lawbearer," he whispered, the name rising unbidden from memory's depths.

Evienne nodded grimly. "Once her divine counterpart. Now her hunter."

***

"What must I do?" Lucan asked.

"Find her," Evienne said, rising with fluid grace. "At the sixth bell, when shadows stretch and the veil between memory and truth thins, she walks the Starlatch Market. Memory-dealers know her face, though they cannot say why their oldest stock responds to her presence."

She moved to one shelf, fingers finding a small vial among hundreds. It contained light that moved like liquid silk. "Drink this when unraveling begins. It will hold your form together long enough to reach her. Use it sparingly."

Lucan accepted the vial, surprised by its warmth. "And then?"

"Then trust what defiance forged and flame sealed." Her smile held sorrow and hope in equal measure. "Soulmarks are not chains but promises made manifest. Some promises are too strong for death, too deep for forgetting, too true for divine law to break."

The third bell tolled in the distance, The Bell of Names, its voice carrying across marsh and stone. Lucan stood, each step requiring conscious effort to remain corporeal.

"Mother Evienne," he said at the threshold, "what was her name? Before?"

The old woman tilted her head, blindfold catching emberlight. "When she remembers her true name, the bonds will sing or shatter. Until then..." She gestured toward the market district. "Until then, she is Caelin Wenriel. Keeper of fragments, restorer of broken things. Both drawn to what needs mending."

***

He left her among emberlight and relics, her words following him into the twisting streets. The soulmark pulsed with each step, pulling him toward the market district where memory-dealers traded in lost dreams, and a woman named Caelin touched glyphs that blazed in recognition of divinity she couldn't remember possessing.

As he rounded the corner where the marsh gave way to cobblestone, a terrible emptiness seized him. His fingers dissolved first, transparency creeping up his arms like frost on glass. The sensation was absence, the void where substance should exist, claiming him inch by inch. A passerby walked through his right shoulder without noticing, sending ripples through his fading form.

With trembling hands, he retrieved Evienne's vial. The liquid light within pulsed in rhythm with his soulmark, responding to his desperation. He uncorked it with fingers that barely maintained form and let a single drop fall onto his tongue. The taste was memory itself, bitter with loss, sweet with recognition. Warmth spread outward from his core, and his flesh solidified once more, though the effort left him gasping against a stone wall.

The golden ring in his eye brightened as afternoon shadows stretched. Somewhere in the city's heart, the sixth bell prepared to call the lost toward each other across the vast distance of forgetting.

# CHAPTER 5
# THE CROSSING

The sixth bell's resonance lingered in the air like a held breath as Caelin gathered her restoration supplies. The Bell of Echoes always unsettled her. Something about its tone made the walls seem to whisper secrets just beyond comprehension. Tonight, the sensation pressed against her consciousness with unusual intensity, as though the city itself urged her toward something she couldn't name.

Heat pulsed beneath her collarbone in rhythm with her heartbeat, more active today than in weeks. Warmth cascaded through her chest with each throb, a sensation both foreign and achingly familiar.

"The memory-glass fragments won't wait around forever." Jalen stood in the workshop doorway, his satchel already stuffed with tools and sketching supplies. His eyes darted nervously to the half-concealed preservation sigil pinned inside his collar, the mark of those who monitored unusual phenomena for the city's safety. "The merchant said they'd only keep them until moonrise."

Caelin carefully fastened her pack, double-checking that her measuring tools rested safely cushioned inside. The Starlatch Market awakened only after sunset, its unusual goods appearing when starlight touched the lanterns tethered with silver chains. Most people avoided it, finding it too bizarre and filled with seemingly impossible items. For restorationists hunting rare materials, however, it remained an indispensable treasure trove.

"I still say we should have brought more coin," Jalen muttered as they descended into the narrow streets winding toward the Lower Eastern Market District. "Memory-glass from the pre-Collapse period doesn't come cheap. And the stories about what people trade for it..." He shivered despite his heavy cloak.

"We have enough." Caelin adjusted her own cloak against the evening chill, though warmth continued radiating from the spot below her throat. The sensation had plagued her all day, flaring without provocation during the most mundane tasks—while cataloging fragments, while mixing preservation solutions, while simply breathing. She wondered, not for the first time, if such sensations had driven the Archives director to station Jalen as her assistant. The Preservation Society seemed increasingly interested in her unusual sensitivity to ancient artifacts.

As they ventured deeper into the market quarter, the streets narrowed. Ancient cobblestones transitioned into pathways that subtly changed when glimpsed from the corner of the eye. Lanterns dangled at improbable angles, their silver chains defying gravity as they swayed to a rhythm matching no earthly breeze. When night fully descended over the eastern quarter of Elowen's Fall, the transformation took hold.

Stalls shimmered into existence like mirages gaining substance. Canvas walls rippled with patterns that hurt to follow directly, geometric designs folding in on themselves in ways that made the eye water. Merchants emerged from shadows that had been empty moments before, their wares spreading across tables that materialized with the weight of captured moonbeams.

"Every time," Jalen said, his voice tight with wonder and unease. "How do they do it? The entire district just...changes."

"Old contracts with the city itself," Caelin replied, though she'd never been certain if that explanation held truth or merely comfort. "Some bargains predate the Collapse. The stones remember agreements that mortal minds have forgotten." She traced a finger along the edge of a nearby wall, feeling the subtle thrum of ancient glyphwork beneath preservation matrices far more complex than anything the modern Preservation Society could recreate.

They moved deeper into the ethereal bazaar, past stalls offering bottled sighs in crystalline vials that hummed with trapped emotion. Names floated like preserved moths in amber jars, their syllables visible as golden script against the glass. Hours stolen from clocks sat heavy as liquid mercury, sold by vendors whose smiles revealed too many teeth.

The air thickened here, charged with possibilities that made the rational mind recoil. Caelin stopped every few steps, drawn by wares that pulsed with recognition when she drew near.

"There." Jalen pointed toward a stall draped in midnight blue silk that rippled like water. "Memory-glass fragments, just as promised."

But Caelin had frozen midstep. The heat beneath her collarbone intensified to an uncomfortable degree, and her vision blurred at the edges. Around them, the market's exotic wares surged with sudden life, as though her presence completed some ancient circuit that had waited centuries to close.

A crystalline wind chime began ringing without breeze, its notes forming harmonies that shimmered like starlight and echoed with sorrow. Preserving jars filled with what looked like liquid emotion swirled faster, their contents reaching toward her through the glass. The silver chains supporting the lanterns vibrated, the market's infrastructure responding to an arrival long expected.

"Caelin?" Jalen's voice reached her from what felt like a great distance. "You've gone chalk white. And the air around you..." He gestured helplessly. "It's shimmering."

A veiled figure materialized beside them, moving with the fluid grace of shadow rather than substance. They had existed here since the market's first breath, feeding on the endless cycle of loss and longing that drew souls to this crossroads between worlds. Their stall held treasures beyond categorization: crystallized tears catching light like diamonds, threads of captured laughter wound on spools of bone, mirrors reflecting memories instead of faces, each item a fragment of someone's discarded essence, carefully harvested and preserved.

"Lose something, friends?" the merchant asked. Multiple voices layered into one, each tone carrying its own weight of sorrow and promise. They existed in symbiosis with the market's ancient hunger, sustained by the raw emotion bleeding from every transaction. "I could sell it back to you. The first try is always free."

***

The offer hung in the air like incense, sweet and cloying. The merchant's power harmonized with the market's heartbeat, drawing forth buried memories and half-forgotten aches. Caelin leaned forward despite her instincts screaming warnings. The warmth beneath her neckline flared in response, filling her mouth with a coppery, electric sensation.

What had she lost? Her dreams of burning wings, the sensation of falling through radiance, and the certainty that someone had stolen something precious suddenly gained new urgency.

"What things do people lose?" she whispered.

The merchant's smile showed even through the veil, stretching too wide for human anatomy, extending beyond facial boundaries. This was their purpose, their addiction, to witness recognition blooming in a customer's eyes, to taste the exquisite pain of remembering what had been forgotten. "Names that sing when spoken. Faces that glow with inner light. The weight of wings spreading wide enough to embrace the sky. The sensation of starlight on a lover's lips. A voice called across impossible distances, its words older than the world itself."

Each phrase struck like a physical blow. Caelin gasped, hand flying to her throat as images exploded behind her eyelids: wings of violet flame spreading against a sky screaming its pain, golden chains breaking with thunderous sound, her own voice speaking words in a language predating mortal speech, the sensation of falling while desperately trying to fly.

The heat beneath her collarbone seared like a brand fresh from the forge. She staggered, vision swimming, and Jalen grabbed her arm in alarm. His eyes widened, less concern than quiet calculation.

"Careful," an unknown voice cut through her vision like a blade through silk. "Some memories exact prices their carriers can't afford."

Caelin's eyes snapped open. A man stood at her other shoulder, tall and lean in worn leathers bearing the dust of distant roads. Dark hair fell across features etched by determination and patient sorrow. When his eyes found hers, she glimpsed something that stole her breath: one eye warm brown, familiar as home, while the other burned with a ring of pale gold flame. Divine retribution stamped on mortal bones.

Recognition hit like lightning, wordless and devastating. She didn't know his face, couldn't recall his name, but something deeper than memory recognized him. The heat beneath her skin erupted into an agony bordering on ecstasy.

"I know you," she breathed, the words torn from her throat.

"Not yet," he replied, voice rough with centuries of waiting. "But you will."

He reached for the same memory-glass fragment she'd been examining. When their fingers brushed, the world exploded.

Violet-gold light erupted between them, outshining the market's ethereal lanterns with celestial brilliance. Beneath her cloak, Caelin's soulmark awakened for the first time, revealing an intricate divine script. The markings spiraled from her shoulder like a living constellation, each glyph radiating violet fire that traced elaborate curves across her skin, winglike patterns etched upon her flesh. The sensation was both excruciating and fulfilling, like discovering a long-sought sanctuary while simultaneously having her heart torn apart.

Around them, every glyph and ward embedded in the market stalls responded, recognizing something they'd awaited centuries to witness. The silver-chained lanterns blazed white-bright, their light bending toward the joined radiance of two souls meeting across an impossible distance. Vendors retreated in awe and terror, while customers throughout the market turned to stare at the column of light rising from their point of contact.

"Impossible," the veiled merchant backed away from their joined illumination. "The twin-marks. I thought those were legends whispered by madmen."

The stranger's features sharpened with desperate hope and carefully contained anguish. His golden-ringed eye blazed like a star, and when he spoke, his voice carried the weight of someone who'd waited too long for this moment.

"You remember in dreams," he whispered, close enough for his words to brush against her ear like a prayer. "The falling, the light that burned through bone and memory. A choice that shattered heaven itself."

The words unlocked something in her mind. For a terrifying moment, she was falling again, violet flame wings streaming behind her like banners of defiance, while above, the sky cracked like glass and rained starfire. She tasted the copper-bright flavor of love so fierce it would break the world rather than be denied.

Caelin jerked away from his touch, severing the blazing connection like a snapped cord. The market held its breath, vendors and customers alike frozen by what they'd witnessed. Her soulmark continued to burn beneath her cloak, traceries of violet-gold light pulsing with her thundering heartbeat.

"Caelin," Jalen's voice cracked with shock, words tumbling out breathlessly. His eyes darted between Caelin's face and the strange new mark. "What is that mark?" His hands trembled as he gestured toward it, fear creeping into his expression. "How long have you had it?" The questions sped up, his voice climbing higher with each word. He took an involuntary step back, then immediately forward again, torn between protective instinct and self-preservation. "What just happened? I mean, really, what the hell just happened?" He ran a shaky hand through his hair. His usual composure had shattered, and beneath it all was the calculating gaze of someone who would report this incident to his superiors.

She couldn't answer. The stranger's golden-ringed eye held her gaze, and in its depths she saw recognition so profound it threatened to shatter what little certainty she'd built around her careful, ordered life.

"Who are you?" she whispered, though part of her feared the answer more than falling.

"Someone who has been looking for you across lifetimes," he replied. Each word carried a precise truth that hurt. "Someone who died rather than let you fall alone."

The words struck with physical force. Caelin felt herself fracturing, the careful walls she'd built around her strange dreams crumbling under the weight of truth she wasn't ready to face. She turned and fled, pushing through the crowd of stunned merchants and wide-eyed customers.

Behind her, Jalen called her name with frantic concern. But the stranger's voice followed her longest, carrying a promise that made her soulmark flare with terrified anticipation:

"I will find you again, Caelin Wenriel. We have too much unfinished between us for time, or forgetting, to keep us apart."

***

As she ran through the market's dissolving edges, violets bloomed in her wake, deep purple petals sprouting impossibly from cold stone, spreading like a living trail of memory through the place where two souls had recognized each other across the vast distance of forgetting.

The market continued its ethereal dance around the space she'd vacated, but something fundamental had shifted. The air vibrated with potential, and those sensitive to such things whispered that magic, long dormant, had awakened.

In the shadow of a silk-draped stall, the stranger stood motionless, watching the path of violets marking her flight. His hand pressed against his chest, where beneath ancient leather a soulmark pulsed in perfect rhythm with the one now blazing beneath her collarbone.

For the first time since awakening in this mortal city whose stones he'd once walked as a guardian, Lucan Thiros allowed himself to hope.

# CHAPTER 6
# THE RECOGNITION

The violets followed her home.

Caelin stumbled through the twisting streets of Elowen's Fall, her breath coming in sharp gasps that had nothing to do with the pace she'd set. Behind her, a trail of unfeasible flowers bloomed from cracks in the ancient cobblestones, their deep purple petals catching starlight like fragments of captured dreams. The fire burning beneath her collarbone pulsed with each frantic heartbeat, a sensation both alien and achingly familiar that spread beneath her skin with inexorable heat.

The merchant called it a twin-mark. Twin soulmarks, forged in defiance and sealed in flame.

That was impossible. She was Caelin Wenriel, restorer of broken things, cataloger of fragments who lived a quiet life among dust and ancient stone. She didn't possess mysterious marks that erupted in violet fire or touch strangers and feel her soul recognize them across unthinkable distances.

***

Her workshop stood dark and welcoming in the eastern quarter, nestled between the Archivist's Tower and the old Preservation Hall. Its familiar outline offered blessed relief after the market's ethereal impossibilities. Caelin fumbled with her key, hands trembling as heat continued radiating through her chest. She needed light, needed to see what had appeared on her skin, needed to understand what was happening to her carefully ordered world.

The door swung shut behind her with a decisive click, and she moved through the workshop's familiar shadows toward her private chambers. The space stretched before her in organized chaos. Long workbenches carved from ancient oak bore the scars of decades of careful restoration, their surfaces stained with preservation oils and marked by the gentle scoring of countless chisels. Shelves lined the walls from floor to ceiling, holding carefully cataloged fragments of stone and metal, each piece tagged with meticulous notes in her precise handwriting.

Glass cabinets protected the most delicate finds: shards of memory-glass that caught the lamplight like trapped stars, pieces of glyph-etched pottery that still hummed with dormant power, and fragments of pre-Collapse metalwork whose purposes had been lost to time. Oil lamps flickered to life under her practiced touch, casting warm circles of light across the room, illuminating dust motes that danced above bins of carefully sorted stone chips and coils of preservation wire.

In the small mirror above her washbasin, Caelin caught her reflection and went still. Her eyes held a distant light that hadn't been there that morning, and her skin seemed to glow with barely contained energy. With trembling fingers, she unpinned her cloak and let it fall.

The soulmark blazed beneath her shoulder like a brand of living fire.

A single glyph, no larger than her palm, burned with violet-gold light just below her left shoulder. The mark's intricate curves formed something that could have been wings spread in flight or flames reaching toward the heavens. The design shifted in her perception, never quite settling into one interpretation. Each line seemed to breathe with a life separate from her own, terrifying and beautiful in equal measure, undeniably part of her yet foreign as divine fire.

"What are you?" she whispered to her reflection, fingers hovering just above the glowing mark. "What am I?"

A sound from the workshop's main room made her freeze. Deliberate footsteps moved between her workbenches with the confidence of someone who belonged. Her heart slammed against her ribs as she grabbed her heaviest chisel from the preparation table. Hardly a weapon but something solid to anchor her courage.

"Caelin." The voice carried through the thin door, rough with exhaustion and something deeper that made her soulmark flare in response. "I know you're frightened. But we need to talk."

She recognized that voice with bone-deep certainty. The stranger from the market, the man whose touch had ignited the mark now burning beneath her skin. Her hand hesitated on the door latch, fingers quivering with the pull between fear and inexplicable longing.

"You're trespassing," she called back, surprised by the steadiness of her own voice.

"Yes," he agreed simply. "But some conversations can't wait for proper invitations."

The honesty in his admission caught her off guard. Most would have offered excuses or justifications. He simply acknowledged the transgression and stood by his choice. Something about that directness, that refusal to hide behind polite fiction, resonated with a part of her she hadn't known existed.

Caelin opened the door.

***

He stood near her main workbench, examining a fragment of pre-Collapse stonework with the careful attention of someone who understood its true value. In the lamplight, his features carried a stark beauty, sharp cheekbones shadowed by fatigue, a mouth that spoke of both gentleness and determination, dark hair that fell across his forehead in a way that made her fingers itch to brush it back. The golden ring circling his right iris caught the light, burning with an inner fire that spoke of divine judgment worn like a scar.

But it was his stillness that unsettled her the most. He breathed, but the rhythm seemed deliberate rather than natural. He moved with fluid grace, but shadows pooled strangely around him, as though light couldn't quite decide if he was solid enough to block it.

"My name is Lucan Thiros," he said without looking up from the stone fragment, his voice carrying depths that suggested far more years than his appearance showed. "And I've been waiting for you for longer than I can intone."

"That's impossible." But even as she spoke the words, Caelin felt their falseness. Nothing about this night followed the rules of possibility.

"Many unimaginable things have proven true lately." He set the fragment down with reverent care and turned to face her fully. When his gaze found hers, she glimpsed desperate hope carefully contained beneath patient sorrow. "The return of the dead. Dreams that bleed into waking. Flowers growing from stone." His attention dropped to where her soulmark glowed beneath the thin fabric of her shirt, and heat flared along her skin in response. "The manifestation of bonds thought lost to time itself."

"What are these marks?" The question emerged as barely a whisper.

Instead of answering with words, Lucan began unlacing his leather jerkin with deliberate movements. Caelin's breath caught as he revealed the broad expanse of his chest, pale skin marked by old scars and something far more significant. There, directly over his heart, an identical soulmark blazed with gold fire. The glyph was a single intricate design of interwoven curves that formed the suggestion of both wings and flame, creating a pattern that perfectly complemented the one adorning her shoulder. Two halves of a whole, divided and now reunited.

"Twin-forged soulmarks," he explained, his voice rougher than before as he watched her study the glowing script. "Bonds created when two souls choose each other so completely that the choice rewrites reality itself." He pressed his palm flat against his mark, and hers flared in immediate response, the connection singing between them like struck metal. "They were forged centuries ago, in defiance of laws both divine and mortal."

"Centuries?" Caelin's voice cracked on the word. Her knees weakened, and she gripped the doorframe for support. "That's illogical. I'm barely thirty, and you..." She studied his face again, noting the timeless quality of his features that belonged to old paintings rather than living men.

"I died close to a millennium ago," he said with devastating simplicity. "The bond brought me back. Not fully alive, not truly dead, but something suspended between states, sustained only by the connection to your soul."

The revenant condition. She'd read fragments about such beings in the oldest texts, but even the Preservation Society's scholars considered them myth. Her fingers tightened on the doorframe as her mind struggled to categorize this impossibility standing before her.

"You're saying I'm bound to a ghost."

"Not a ghost." His smile carried bitter edges that spoke of centuries spent questioning his own nature. "Something closer to a revenant, though the distinction matters little. What matters is this: my existence depends on the strength of our bond. Each day you don't remember weakens the connection that holds me together. Each moment of doubt unravels another thread keeping me anchored to form."

As if summoned by his words, his form flickered at the edges like a candle guttering in the wind. For a terrifying instant, she could see through his hand to the workbench beyond, his substance becoming as translucent as old glass before flesh reasserted itself with visible effort. The strain of maintaining coherence creased his face, evidence of the constant battle he fought simply to exist.

"You're fading," she breathed, instinctively stepping closer as though proximity might stabilize whatever force kept him coherent.

"Returning to whatever realm claims the forgotten dead." Color returned to his features as she approached. "Unless..."

"Unless what?"

"Unless you choose to remember. To reclaim what they took from you." His gaze held hers, unflinching but without pressure. "But that choice has to be freely made. I can't force memory to return, can't compel recognition through will alone. All I can do is show you fragments and hope they resonate with something deeper than conscious thought."

Caelin moved closer without conscious decision, drawn by the careful reverence in his voice and the answering fire building in her chest. The space between them hummed with potential, electric and undeniable. Something in her recognized him beyond rational thought, a knowing that preceded memory. She'd spent her life believing in tangible evidence, in fragments that could be cataloged and restored, yet this certainty defied such methodical analysis.

"Show me," she said.

Lucan gestured toward an intricate glyph carved into her workbench, pre-Collapse craftsmanship that had always responded to her touch with unusual enthusiasm. "This is a memory-binding, designed to preserve moments of intense significance. Place your hand on it while I do the same. If our bonds recognize each other..."

She pressed her palm flat against the carved stone, feeling its familiar warmth respond to her touch like a heart finding its rhythm. Lucan's hand covered hers, his skin fever warm where it made contact, and the moment their flesh joined, the world exploded into memory.

***

For a terrifying moment, she was falling again, wings of violet flame streaming behind her like banners of defiance, while above, the sky cracked like glass and rained starfire.

But deeper than the falling, another memory surfaced, intimate and devastating.

A hidden garden carpeted with violets, their purple blooms soft as silk beneath her bare shoulders. Lucan's hands mapping the luminous contours of her divine form while starlight traced silver patterns across his mortal skin. The sensation of his lips against the hollow of her throat where celestial fire pulsed like a second heartbeat, his breath catching as her wings spread to shelter them both from heaven's watching eyes. The exquisite transgression of divine flesh yielding to mortal touch, the way he whispered her true name like a prayer against her collarbone while violet petals clung to their entwined limbs. How her light had poured through him in that moment of joining, making his eyes blaze with reflected divine fire as their souls forged something unprecedented, a bond that would survive death itself.

The garden memory dissolved, replaced by another moment of equal intensity...

Starlight woven into hair that cascaded like liquid silk down bare shoulders. Wings of violet flame spreading against a twilight sky, their span vast enough to embrace mountains. Her own voice, speaking words in a language older than human speech. "I choose love over law, devotion over duty. Let heaven itself break before this bond does, and let the earth remember what the sky forgets."

Strong hands clasping hers as vows flowed between them like molten gold, sealing promises that made the air itself sing with power. The sensation of divinity beyond mortal comprehension flowing through the connection, celestial nature responding to mortal love with explosive force that cracked reality like struck glass.

And then falling, falling through light that burned away everything but choice itself, wings crumbling to ash as divinity bled from mortal flesh in streams of violet fire while above, the sky screamed its protest across all the realms.

The vision shattered like breaking crystal, leaving Caelin gasping against Lucan's chest. Her hands fisted in his jerkin as the workshop re-formed around them. The soulmark beneath her skin sang with recognition, each glyph burning so brightly the light shone through her shirt in traceries of celestial fire. She could feel his heart beating beneath her palm, or perhaps that was her own pulse, magnified by proximity until she couldn't distinguish between them.

***

"Did you see?" Lucan's voice rumbled against her ear.

"Wings," she whispered, the word torn from her throat like a prayer. "I had wings. And you..." She lifted her head to meet his gaze, finding herself close enough to count the gold flecks in his dark eye. "You were there when I fell."

"I tried to catch you." His thumb traced along her jaw with heartbreaking gentleness. "I died trying, and I failed."

The admission carried such a weight of sorrow that Caelin felt something crack open in her chest. Without thinking, she reached up to touch his face near the golden ring, watching him shudder at the contact, eye fluttering closed as though her touch brought either pain or absolution.

"What is this mark?"

"Divine judgment," he said, voice thick with old shame. "Placed by those who said a mortal had no right to love divinity. That I presumed too much in thinking myself worthy of such a bond, of you."

"And do you?" The question slipped out before she could stop it, intimate and essential. "Think yourself worthy?"

His eyes opened, and she glimpsed a vulnerability so raw it stole her breath. "I've had centuries to question that. To wonder if their judgment was correct, if I doomed us both through selfish desire that couldn't accept the natural order." His hand covered hers where it rested against his cheek, the contact sending sparks racing along her nerves. "But then I touch you, and the mark burns less. As though your presence argues for my worthiness when I cannot."

The tenderness in his voice, the careful reverence in his touch, made something deep in her unfurl like flower petals seeking the sun. This felt familiar in ways that transcended memory, the shape of his hands, the cadence of his breathing when he held her close, the way he touched her as though she were spun starlight that could slip through his fingers if he wasn't careful enough.

"I don't remember loving you," she said, watching something flicker across his expression that might have been pain. "But I recognize being loved. Being seen and chosen and cherished beyond reason or law."

"That's enough," he breathed, relief transforming his features. "For now, that's more than enough."

A sharp knock at the workshop door shattered the moment's intimacy. Caelin jerked back from Lucan's touch, immediately missing the connection's warmth as cold air rushed between them.

"Caelin?" Jalen's voice carried concern and confusion in equal measure. "Are you in there? You left the market so suddenly, and I've been worried sick. There are violets growing throughout the streets you walked, impossible things, blooming from solid stone, and people are saying..." His voice trailed off, then strengthened with determination. "Well, they're saying impossible things."

Lucan moved as though to step back into the shadows, but Caelin caught his wrist before he could retreat. The contact sent fire racing through her veins, and his form solidified under her touch, color flooding back into his features.

"Stay," she said, decision crystallizing even as she spoke. "If we're bound as you claim, then hiding serves no purpose."

"Your friend may not react well to learning his colleague converses with the returned dead." Lucan's expression darkened. "Some in this city have made careers of containing what they consider dangerous manifestations."

The subtle warning made her pause. "You mean the Preservation Society?"

"There are those within it who serve a different master, the Order of Preservation. They've worked for centuries to prevent another Collapse, by any means necessary."

Caelin frowned, connecting fragments of overheard conversations and odd behaviors she'd noticed among certain senior preservationists. "And Jalen?"

"I don't know where his loyalties lie," Lucan admitted. "But caution would be wise."

She considered this, then squeezed his wrist once before releasing him. "Then we'll be cautious."

***

When she opened the door, Jalen almost stumbled over his own feet in his eagerness to see past her into the workshop. His sandy hair was even more disheveled than usual, and ink stained his sleeves nearly to the elbows from hasty note-taking.

"Thank the ancestors," he breathed, relief clear in every line of his posture. "When you disappeared like that, I thought something terrible had happened. The market dissolved into chaos after you left, vendors packing up their stalls like they'd witnessed something they weren't prepared to handle." His gaze moved past her to Lucan, and his expression shifted to puzzled recognition mixed with growing alarm. "You! You were at the market. The moment you both touched the memory-glass, Caelin and you..." He trailed off, gesturing between them. "What happened back there? The light from your skin, those flowers blooming in your wake. None of it follows any preservation theory I've studied."

"Some phenomena exist beyond the scope of standard theories," Lucan replied with careful diplomacy. "Particularly when dealing with pre-Collapse artifacts and their...unexpected reactions to certain bloodlines."

Jalen's eyes narrowed as he studied Lucan with the intensity of someone trained to catalog mysteries and identify their origins. His hand drifted unconsciously to the inner pocket of his coat, where Caelin knew he kept his official Preservation Society notebook.

"You speak like you've encountered such reactions before. Your knowledge of ancient glyphwork was precise for a casual observer."

"I've had extensive exposure to the Archives and their contents," Lucan said, which carried truth without revealing the full extent of his experience.

"And that mark in your eye?" Jalen pressed, catching the subtle evasions. His scholarly curiosity warred with something deeper, a flicker of conflict that suggested knowledge beyond what he'd admitted. "That's not natural. Or normal. And the way you moved through that crowd, people stepped aside without looking, as though something in them recognized..." He swallowed hard. "What are you?"

Before Lucan could respond, Caelin stepped forward, drawing Jalen's attention to her own transformed state. In the workshop's lamplight, her soulmark glowed through the thin fabric of her shirt, its violet script pulsing with each heartbeat.

"Neither is this," she said, watching Jalen's expression cycle from shock to fascination to something approaching fear. "Whatever's happening is larger than theories or normal explanations."

Jalen stared at the mark with mounting excitement that gradually overwhelmed his caution. He stepped closer to examine the details of the glyph, but something in his eyes suggested divided attention, as though part of him assessed the situation through a different lens than mere academic interest.

"Incredible. The complexity of the script, the way it moves like living flame... Caelin, this could revolutionize our understanding of pre-Collapse glyphwork." He pulled out his ever-present notebook, stylus already moving. "May I document it? Take detailed sketches? The Preservation Society needs to know about this discovery immediately."

"No." The word emerged harder than she'd intended, backed by an instinct that insisted privacy mattered more than academic advancement. "This isn't for cataloging or study. It's..." She glanced at Lucan, who watched her with careful hope. "It's personal."

Jalen's crestfallen expression made guilt twist in her chest. He'd been nothing but kind to her, welcoming her enthusiasm for restoration when others found her intensity off-putting. But the way his eyes had darted between Lucan and her mark, calculating rather than simply curious, it reinforced Lucan's warning.

"I understand," Jalen said, though his tone suggested he didn't. He tucked his notebook away with obvious reluctance. "But, Caelin, please be careful. Phenomena like this, bonds and marks that appear without explanation... They can carry a price not as apparent to those who bear them." His gaze flicked to Lucan with a meaning that seemed almost like a warning. "Those who've studied the Collapse know that divine manifestations always come at a cost."

"All worthwhile bonds carry risk," Lucan said, his voice carrying the weight of someone who'd paid such prices and found them acceptable. "The question becomes whether the connection justifies the cost."

A shadow passed over Jalen's face. There and gone so quickly, Caelin almost missed it, a fleeting expression that suggested personal knowledge of such calculations. For a moment, she glimpsed not the enthusiastic scholar but someone carrying heavier burdens than he'd ever revealed.

"Sometimes we don't know the true cost until it's too late to choose differently," Jalen murmured, then seemed to catch himself. He forced a smile that didn't quite reach his eyes. "But that's a conversation for scholars in their cups, not for tonight. I should go."

As Jalen turned to leave, Caelin glimpsed something tucked in his inner pocket, not the familiar Preservation Society notebook with its blue binding, but something bound in worn black leather bearing a symbol she'd never seen before. The brief glimpse sent an inexplicable chill down her spine.

"Stay," she said to Lucan as Jalen prepared to leave, the word slipping out before conscious thought could intervene. "Tonight. In the workshop. I have questions that can't wait for proper timing."

Surprise flickered across his features, followed by something that might have been profound relief. "Are you certain?"

"Nothing about this night has dealt in certainties," she replied, aware of Jalen's sharp attention. "But I'm tired of running from mysteries that follow me home regardless of how fast I flee."

Jalen cleared his throat diplomatically. "I should return to my workshop. Process today's...unusual experiences." He paused at the threshold, expression serious despite his obvious curiosity. "Caelin? Whatever this is, whatever you're dealing with, you're not alone. If you need someone to research farfetched theories, to listen to explanations that defy reason..." He shrugged with forced lightness. "I've grown rather fond of implausible things."

When Jalen's footsteps faded into the night, silence settled over the workshop like a held breath. Caelin found herself hyperaware of Lucan's presence behind her. The quiet rhythm of breathing he didn't need, the warmth that radiated from his skin despite his not-quite-living state, the way her soulmark responded whenever he moved closer.

***

"Your friend is more than he appears," Lucan said quietly, watching the door as though he could still see Jalen through it.

"What do you mean?"

"He studies you with divided interest, genuine affection tempered by something more calculated." Lucan's expression softened. "Though I sense his conflict about it, which speaks well of his character."

Caelin thought of the hidden black notebook, of Jalen's strange reactions and pointed questions. "Do you think he means me harm?"

"Not intentionally. But loyalty to the wrong people can become its own kind of danger." Lucan's gaze returned to her, warming. "You said you had questions."

"With the truth," she said. "All of it. What we were, what we chose, and what it cost us both."

"That's a long story," he warned, settling into the chair beside her workbench with movements that suggested his existence remained more fragile than it appeared. "And not all of it will be pleasant to hear."

"I'm beginning to suspect that the pleasant stories don't leave marks like these." She touched her collarbone where the soulmark pulsed with patient fire. "Tell me anyway."

***

Outside, violets continued blooming in the wake of their recognition, and somewhere in the distance, the eighth bell, the Bell of Quiet, began its slow toll toward midnight. As Lucan spoke, his voice carrying the weight of centuries and choices that had shattered the sky itself, Caelin leaned closer, drawn by the promise of answers to questions she hadn't known she'd been carrying her entire life.

In the shadows beyond her workshop, a figure lingered, watching the warm glow of lamplight through her windows. Jalen's expression was torn between duty and friendship as he opened the black leather book and began to write. His report to the Order of Preservation was already forming in precise, troubled script.

The truth, whatever it held, was finally within reach. And its consequences wouldn't wait long to find them.

# Chapter 7
# The Ashwell

T he dreams no longer waited for sleep.

Caelin jerked awake as violet fire blazed behind her eyelids, her mouth flooding with the metallic sensation of starlight while phantom wings pressed against her shoulder blades with bruising intensity. The sensation appeared so real she twisted to check her back, fingers searching for feathers that weren't there, for divinity that had burned away centuries ago.

Beside her workbench, where Lucan had kept vigil through the night, dawn's cruel light revealed what darkness had hidden. His form flickered like a candle starved of oxygen, edges blurring until she could see the wooden chair through his chest, the wall through his hands. Each breath he took seemed deliberate rather than necessary, as though he had to remember how to exist with each moment that passed.

"You're disappearing," she whispered, the words scraping her throat raw.

"Dawn weakens the connection," he admitted, voice hollow with the effort of maintained coherence. His marked eye had dimmed from gold fire to pale amber, the divine judgment wearing thin. "Night brings dreams closer to the surface. Dreams strengthen the bond between us. But morning..." He gestured at his translucent hand, watching light pass through flesh that should have been solid. "Morning reminds me what I am. A ghost sustained by borrowed memory."

Terror clawed at her chest. Without thinking, Caelin lunged from the narrow cot she'd dragged into the workshop, reaching for him with desperate hands. The moment her fingers brushed his cheek, substance reasserted itself beneath her touch. Color flooded back through his form like water soaking into parched earth, and she found warm skin and the sharp line of bone beneath her fingers.

His breath hitched, unnecessary but achingly human, and his eyes closed as though her touch brought salvation and torment in equal measure.

"Better," she breathed, thumb tracing the gold ring that marked his eye with divine judgment. The intimacy of the gesture should have seemed foreign. Instead, it carried the weight of muscle memory, a pattern her hands knew even when her mind couldn't recall learning it.

"I can't survive on borrowed touches forever," Lucan said, though he leaned into her caress like a man starving for warmth. "The bond grows weaker each day you remain uncertain. Soon even contact won't be enough to anchor me to this form."

"Then I need answers." Her fingers curled into fists at her sides, nails biting into the palms. Decision crystallized in her chest like ice forming on still water. "Real ones. Not fragments glimpsed through broken memory-glass or half-remembered dreams bleeding into waking hours. I need to understand what I was, what we chose, and what it cost us both."

"The visions you've been having—"

"Aren't enough." She stood, pacing to the window where dawn painted Elowen's Fall in shades of gold and ash. In the distance, smoke rose from the bakers' chimneys and the first market criers began their calls, the city waking to another day of careful normalcy. How could they continue their mundane routines when reality itself seemed fractured?

The thought terrified her. This wasn't just about strange dreams or unusual abilities anymore. Something fundamental was changing within her, reshaping her understanding of herself. Each recovered memory fragment threatened to overwhelm her identity as Caelin. What if seeking more meant losing herself entirely?

"I'm afraid," she admitted, the words barely audible. "Afraid that whatever I discover will erase who I am now. But I'm more afraid of watching you fade while I cling to safe ignorance."

Lucan rose with careful precision, each movement deliberate, as though his joints had forgotten how to work in harmony. In the morning light, shadows pooled strangely around him, uncertain whether he cast them or they cast him into existence.

"Where will you seek these answers?"

"The Ashwell." The name emerged from some deep place in her consciousness, carrying certainty despite never having spoken it before. Knowledge surfaced like bubbles rising through dark water: obsidian stone, silver tears, water that showed truth to those brave enough to look. "North of the city, where memory bleeds through stone and the blessed dead whisper secrets to the living."

His marked eye flared with something between desperate hope and alarm. "The Ashwell doesn't offer gentle revelations, Caelin. What it shows can shatter minds unprepared for the memory. The Ashwell has left mortals rocking and speaking in prehuman tongues days later, their minds shattered by what it revealed."

"Then it's convenient I'm not entirely mortal anymore." She touched the spot where her soulmark burned beneath her shirt, considering its steady pulse like a second heartbeat, stronger now than her first. "Whatever I am now, whatever I'm becoming, staying ignorant serves no purpose. You're dying by degrees while I cling to safe uncertainty, and I can't save you without understanding what truly binds us."

"Let me come with you."

"No." The refusal emerged harder than intended, but she couldn't soften it. This felt like something she needed to face alone, a confrontation with herself that required absolute solitude. "Your form is too unstable for the journey. And..." She hesitated, searching for words to explain instinct that ran deeper than reason. "This feels like something I have to choose without influence. Even yours."

Pain flickered across his features before he could mask it. "You think my presence would compromise your judgment?"

"I think you've already made your choice," she said, stepping close enough to perceive warmth radiating from his skin when he was solid, the absence of it when he wasn't. "You've waited centuries, died for it, and clawed your way back from whatever lies beyond death's threshold. The weight of your devotion, your centuries of faith in what we were...it would bias any revelation I receive."

Understanding dawned in his expression, followed by something that looked like relief. "You're right. I would interpret any vision to preserve what we had rather than accepting what we've become."

"I'll return before sunset," she promised, reaching for her cloak. The autumn air would be cold in the northern woods, and the journey would take most of the day on foot. "This uncertainty ends today."

His form flickered again, transparency creeping in at the edges as anxiety weakened their connection. "Caelin..." Her name emerged like a prayer. "What if what you learn breaks you? What if the truth is more than mortal flesh can bear?"

"Then I'll break," she said simply, fastening her cloak with practiced movements. "But I'd rather shatter from truth than die slowly of ignorance. And Lucan?" She met his gaze, seeing centuries of patient devotion burning in depths that held more sorrow than any mortal heart should carry. "If I break, I trust you to help me put the pieces back together."

As she turned to leave, she glimpsed something in the room's corner, a shadow that didn't quite match Lucan's movements, watching with quiet intensity. The sight vanished so quickly she might have imagined it, but the impression lingered; something else was connected to Lucan, something that observed from a distance, waiting.

***

The path north wound through stands of silver birch and ancient oak, their branches heavy with morning mist that clung like spectral fingers. As Caelin walked, the city's sounds faded behind her, replaced by the whisper of wind through leaves and the distant call of crows that sounded almost like voices speaking in forgotten languages.

Three times she passed travelers heading toward Elowen's Fall, and three times they averted their eyes without greeting. Something in her countenance must have changed, marking her as different. As she crossed a small stream that divided the cultivated lands from the deeper woods, she caught her reflection in the clear water. Her eyes held a violet shimmer that hadn't been there before, barely perceptible but undeniably present.

Overhead, a hawk circled with unusual persistence, its pattern too regular for natural hunting. Caelin remembered stories of the Order of Preservation using trained birds to track anomalies in the wilderness surrounding the city. The Preservation Society's public face might focus on artifact restoration, but whispers suggested a deeper purpose: monitoring and containing anything that threatened to disrupt the delicate balance established after the Collapse.

The grove announced itself long before she saw it. The air grew thick with the scent of something that might have been incense or might have been sorrow given form. Silver light filtered through branches that swayed without wind and beneath her feet the path changed from packed earth to stones that hummed with residual power.

Then the trees parted, and she saw them.

***

The grove of weeping trees appeared between one step and the next, as though the forest had been waiting for her to prove worthy of its mysteries. Ancient willows formed a perfect circle around a clearing that appeared older than the bones of the earth. Their silver-green branches drooped toward the ground in eternal mourning, and from each hanging limb, tears fell in constant streams, not sap or dew, but actual tears of crystalline silver that caught the filtered light like captured prayers.

The sound of their falling created a constant whisper, syllables in languages that predated human speech. Listening too closely made her mind reel with half-understood meaning, words that spoke of loss and hope and choices that echoed across eternity.

At the grove's heart, the Ashwell waited.

Obsidian formed the shrine's foundation. Black stone lined with veins of gold that pulsed with their own inner light like the heartbeat of sleeping gods. The basin itself was deceptively simple: a perfect circle carved from a single piece of midnight-dark stone, filled with water so black it might have been liquid shadow. But as Caelin approached, golden motes began swimming through the depths, tracing patterns of light that responded to her presence with eager recognition.

"Another seeker comes to the Well of Truth."

The voice belonged to an elderly woman who emerged from behind the largest weeping tree like mist given human form. Her hair hung silver white past her shoulders, unbound and decorated with threads that caught light like spun moonbeams. Her eyes held depths that spoke of seeing too much, knowing too much, carrying burdens that would crush lesser souls. Ritual scars marked her arms in patterns that echoed the golden veins in the obsidian, and when she moved, silver bangles chimed with the same whispered rhythm as the falling tears.

"I am Keeper Miraleth," she continued, settling onto a moss-covered stone beside the well with movements that suggested she'd held this vigil for decades. "I tend the Ashwell's needs and warn those who would drink from its wisdom." Her ancient gaze found Caelin's, sharp with recognition that made the air between them shimmer. "Though I suspect warnings matter little to one who carries starlight in her bones and divine fire beneath her skin."

"You can see what I am?"

"I can see what you're becoming." Miraleth gestured toward the well, where the golden motes swirled faster in response to Caelin's proximity, forming spirals and whorls that tugged at the edges of vanished memory. "The water recognizes divinity, even when wrapped in mortal flesh and sealed behind walls of forgetting. But beware, young catalyst. The Ashwell shows truth without mercy or filter. What you learn may break you entirely before it offers any hope of healing."

"I'm already breaking," Caelin admitted, kneeling beside the basin on stones that held warmth despite the morning chill. Up close, she could see that the golden lights moved with purpose, forming symbols that flickered at the edge of recognition. Divine script, written in illumination on darkness. "The question is not if I will break, but if I will break irretrievably, or into something new and stronger."

"A wise distinction." Miraleth's approval carried the weight of someone who'd watched countless souls face this choice. "Then make your offering, daughter of choice and flame. The well accepts only what carries the deepest truth. Tears, blood, years of life freely given. What do you offer for the sight you seek?"

Caelin stared into the black depths, watching light dance through the darkness in configurations that seemed achingly familiar. Without conscious decision, tears began streaming down her cheeks, not grief exactly but something deeper. The soul recognizing what it had lost, mourning what it couldn't remember.

"I offer sorrow," she whispered, letting the tears fall onto the well's perfectly still surface. Each drop struck the water like a bell, sending ripples of light racing outward from the point of contact. "For choices I don't remember making. For love I can't recall knowing. For wings I've never spread and still mourn losing every time I dream."

The moment her tears touched the water, the world exploded.

Light erupted from the well, not golden but silver-bright, searing and terrible and achingly beautiful. Reality dissolved around her as vision consumed everything she thought she knew about herself, about the ordered universe, and about the careful boundaries between mortal and divine.

She stood in a hall of living starlight, wings of violet flame spreading from her shoulders with a span vast enough to embrace mountains. The sensation of flight sang in her bones, the intoxication of limitless sky and wind that tasted of eternity. Beside her, another figure blazed with silver fire, their beauty too terrible for mortal eyes to perceive directly. When they spoke, reality rewrote itself around their words, bending to accommodate truths too large for creation to contain naturally.

"Sister." The voice cut through her consciousness like benediction and blade combined. "Memory-keeper to my Lawbearer. Choice to my balance. You would fracture our harmony for mortal flesh?"

The figure's name surfaced in her consciousness like something rising from deep water: Nerien. Twin-forged, born from the same divine syllable, created to embody the eternal tension between memory and law. Together, they had been the Chorus, holding reality in perfect balance through their combined aspects, turning the great wheel of existence with their shared purpose.

"I choose love over law," her own voice replied, words carrying the weight of absolute conviction that shook the foundations of heaven itself. "I choose growth over stagnation, possibility over certainty. I choose to cherish over remaining merely perfect."

"You choose chaos." Nerien's form blazed brighter, silver fire streaming from their wings like tears of molten light. Their pain was palpable, radiating through the celestial realm like a wound in the fabric of existence. "You choose destruction for the sake of sensation. Do you understand what your fracturing will unleash?"

She understood. The vision showed her everything: reality cracking along divine fault lines, the careful order of heaven and earth dissolving into chaos, and mortal realms convulsing as the laws that governed them rewrote themselves around her choice. Stars dying as their orbits destabilized. Time fracturing into fragments that fell like broken glass through the void. The screams of a universe learning to exist without the harmony that had shaped it since the first word was spoken.

And she chose it anyway.

"I choose to fall rather than forget," Elowen declared, spreading her wings against the silver storm of Nerien's anguish. Her voice rang with power that shattered the distant constellations. "I choose love that defies gravity like falling stars over duty that leaves us cold as distant light. I choose him."

"Then fall," Nerien whispered, their voice breaking with millennia of accumulated sorrow. "Fall, and forget, and live small and safe and mortal. When you remember what this cost us both, we will speak again. And next time, sister, I will not be so merciful."

The vision shifted with brutal speed, showing her the moment of impact. Wings burning away like tissue paper in a forge, each feather dissolving into sparks of violet fire that fell like dying stars. Divinity streaming from her mortal form in ribbons of light while her body plummeted toward earth that rose to meet her like an enemy. Lucan's desperate attempt to catch her, his body breaking under the weight of falling godhood, bones snapping like twigs as divine fire poured through him. The taste of earth and blood in her mouth as consciousness faded, and above, the sound of heaven screaming its protest at love that refused to bow.

But deeper than the falling, another image surfaced. Nerien catching her divine essence as it fled her broken form, silver hands weaving forgetting like a shroud around her dying light. Not cruelty but mercy, erasing the memory to spare her the agony of understanding what she'd lost, what she'd chosen, what the universe had paid for her moment of selfish love.

"Sleep," they whispered across the vision, their voice thick with tears that fell like rain across the shattered realms. "Sleep and forget and be human. I will carry our burden alone rather than watch you break beneath its weight."

***

The well's surface exploded outward like a geyser. Black water and golden light cascaded across the shrine's obsidian foundation. Caelin screamed as divine memory crashed into mortal flesh, her body convulsing as it tried to contain experiences too vast for human consciousness. Her wings spread in phantom agony, seeking a sky that no longer recognized her right to claim it. Heat blazed beneath her skin as her soulmark tried desperately to contain the overflow of celestial fire.

Through the chaos of returned memory, she thought herself breaking apart, mortal identity dissolving under the weight of what she had been. She was falling again, not through the sky but through the layers of herself, past Caelin the restorer, past human concerns and earthly attachments, toward something vast and terrible and absolutely true.

Strong hands caught her shoulders, grounding her in warmth and desperate familiarity.

"Caelin," Lucan's voice cut through the maelstrom like an anchor, calling her back from dissolution. "You're here. You're safe. The vision is ending."

She opened eyes she didn't remember closing, finding his face inches from her own. His marked eye blazed with concern, the golden ring flaring as he searched her features for signs of permanent damage. Around them, the grove of weeping trees swayed with wind that carried the scent of ozone and burned starlight.

"I felt you breaking across the bond," he said, hands framing her face with heartbreaking gentleness. His touch was solid now, completely substantial, as though her crisis had strengthened their connection. "Your pain came through like fire, like—"

"Like falling," she finished, her voice hoarse from screaming she didn't recall. "I remember falling. I remember choosing it. I remember..." The weight of recovered memory pressed against her mind like a physical force. "I remember what I was. What we did. What it cost."

His breath caught. "Do you remember why?"

"Love," she whispered, the word carrying the weight of absolute certainty. "Love that broke the laws of heaven itself. Love that shattered the balance between order and chaos because I couldn't bear to exist without it, without you." Her hands found his face, fingers tracing the mark placed as judgment for daring to love divinity. "They called you presumptuous. Called our love a contamination of divine purpose."

"And was it worth it?" The question emerged barely above a breath, centuries of doubt and hope hanging in the balance of her answer.

Caelin stared into his eyes, one brown as earth, one ringed with divine fire, and felt something settle into place like a key finding its lock. Not memory returned, but choice renewed. Not because she remembered loving him, but because she could see what loving him had cost and found the price acceptable.

"Ask me again when I've finished putting myself back together," she said, managing something that might have been a smile. "But, Lucan? The answer will be yes."

He pulled her against his chest with desperate relief, arms wrapping around her as though she might dissolve again if he didn't hold tight enough. His form felt more solid than it had in days, color flooding back through his features as though her acceptance fed something essential in his nature. For a long moment, they simply held each other while the grove's silver tears fell around them like blessings from gods who had learned to forgive impossible love.

"I need to understand more," Caelin said against his shoulder, breathing in the scent of leather and something deeper that spoke of starlight and eternity. "The vision showed me Nerien, showed me choosing to fall. But there's still so much missing. How did we meet? How did love grow between guardian and seraph? What happened to you when I fell?"

"Memory returns in fragments," he said, pressing his lips to her hair with careful reverence. "Forcing too much too fast causes damage. Better to let it unfold naturally as your mind builds strength to contain it."

"We may not have time for natural unfolding." She pulled back to meet his gaze, noting how his marked eye had dimmed from blazing gold to warm amber, as though her acceptance had healed even divine judgment. "Your form stabilizes when I accept our connection. But it weakens when I doubt or resist. How long do we have before uncertainty becomes irreversible?"

"Days," he admitted, honesty cutting deep between them. "Perhaps a week if you continue choosing to believe, to remember, to accept what we were. But Caelin..." His thumb brushed across her cheekbone, wiping away tears she didn't realize were still falling. "I won't pressure you toward a choice that could destroy what you've built in this life. If the memories are too much, if reclaiming our connection means losing yourself ent irely..."

"Then I'll be lost," she said, surprising them both with the conviction in her voice. "Because whatever I was before, whoever I've become since, some things matter more than self-preservation. You've waited centuries for me to remember, existing in a space between life and death, held together by nothing but faith that our bond could survive even divine erasure. I can be brave enough to try matching that devotion."

The Keeper Miraleth approached with careful steps, her ancient features bright with something that might have been awe. In her hands, she carried a vessel carved from the same golden-veined obsidian as the well, its surface warm with contained light.

"The Ashwell offers gifts to those who survive its visions intact," she said, presenting the vessel with ceremonial gravity. "Water blessed by truth, carrying echoes of what you've seen. When divine memory threatens to overwhelm mortal flesh, a single drop will ground you in present time and prevent the past from consuming the person you've become."

Caelin accepted the vessel with trembling hands, feeling its weight like responsibility made manifest. "Thank you."

"Do not thank me yet," Miraleth warned, her ancient gaze moving between Caelin and Lucan with the sharpness of someone who recognized forces beyond her experience. "Truth revealed demands choice made. The Ashwell shows what was.

Only you can decide what will be. And, child?" Her voice dropped to barely above a whisper. "Some loves are strong enough to break heaven once. But breaking it twice..." She shook her head. "That may shatter more than can be repaired."

***

Her gaze shifted toward the tree line, where shadows seemed to gather with unusual density. "The Order watches. They sense the awakening of old power, the stirring of forces they've sworn to contain. Your journey home will not be unobserved."

As they walked back through the grove of weeping tears, Lucan's hand warm and solid in hers, Caelin felt the weight of the approaching decision settle around her shoulders like wings she'd forgotten how to use. The vision had shown her the choice that broke heaven once before, love chosen over law, passion over duty, growth over stagnation.

Soon, she would have to decide.

The question was: Would either of them survive what came next?

In the lengthening shadows of afternoon, a hawk still circled overhead, its flight pattern too deliberate to be natural. And deeper in the woods, just beyond the edge of perception, something moved with purpose, watchers who carried the emblem of scales and memory-glass, their robes the color of twilight.

The Order of Preservation had taken notice, and they were not known for their mercy toward those who threatened the delicate balance established after the Collapse.

# CHAPTER 8
# THE BOND

The journey back to Elowen's Fall passed in contemplative silence. Caelin studied Lucan's profile as they walked the forest path, noting details that memories from the Ashwell made achingly familiar. The sharp line of his jaw caught the afternoon light in a way that stirred something deeper than recognition. The careful rhythm of his breathing seemed too deliberate, as though he had to remind himself of such mortal necessities. Most unsettling of all were the shadows that pooled strangely around his form, uncertain whether he cast them or they cast him.

"The visions from the Ashwell," she said as they descended through stands of silver birch toward the city's outskirts, "sometimes they feel more real than my own memories. As though Caelin Wenriel is the dream and Elowen is trying to wake up."

"That's the danger." His marked eye caught the last rays of sunlight filtering through the canopy, the golden ring pulsing with its own inner fire. "Divine memory carries weight that can crush mortal consciousness."

His form flickered slightly at the edges, a momentary transparency that sent an alarm through her. The soulmark beneath her collarbone responded with a sharp heat, as though sensing his instability.

"Is that what happened to you? When you returned from death?" she asked, instinctively moving closer.

His step faltered, shadows wavering around him like disturbed water. "I came back incomplete. Part of me remained wherever the dead go when they surrender to the final darkness." His voice roughened. "What you see now is a fragment sustained by the bond alone."

The stark honesty carved something hollow in her chest. She stopped walking entirely, turning to study his face as he gazed toward the city's distant spires. Where sunlight touched him his skin appeared almost translucent, revealing the faintest outline of bone beneath.

"How much of you is missing?"

"I don't know," he admitted, the words rough with acceptance. "Enough that I sometimes forget entirely about mortal needs—food, sleep, warmth. Enough that I move through crowds and people step aside without conscious thought." His expression shifted, vulnerability bleeding through careful control. "But when you touch me..."

Her soulmark flared with sudden heat, responding to the raw need in his voice. Without conscious decision, she reached for his hand. Their fingers intertwined with the fluid ease of long practice, muscle memory bypassing rational thought entirely.

The transformation was instantaneous and profound. Color flooded his features like water soaking into parched earth. His breathing deepened from deliberate mimicry to natural rhythm. Most remarkably, his shadow solidified beneath him, no longer that eerie pooling of uncertain darkness but the crisp outline of a living man blocking afternoon light.

"Yes," he breathed, relief clear in his expression as he studied their joined hands. "Exactly like that."

***

They completed the walk to Elowen's Fall in comfortable quiet, but instead of approaching the main gates where guards might note his unusual nature, Lucan guided her through narrow alleys that twisted between buildings so old their foundations remembered different names for the city itself.

"Where are we going?" she asked as they navigated passages barely wide enough for a single person.

"Somewhere we can speak without being overheard," he replied, leading her to a door marked only by symbols that rearranged themselves when viewed directly. "Your workshop is being watched."

Ice formed in her stomach. "Watched? By whom?"

"Those who erased your memory the first time." His hand moved to the door's center, pressing against a glyph that flared with gold recognition. "They circle the edges of your awareness even now, testing how much you remember, how strong our connection grows."

As the door swung open, his outline momentarily blurred again, as though the effort of maintaining form taxed whatever energy sustained him.

The space beyond the threshold defied every expectation. The main room stretched wide and welcoming, its vaulted ceiling supported by beams carved with protective symbols that pulsed with patient light. Bookshelves lined every wall, holding volumes whose very letters seemed to move when glimpsed peripherally. A fire crackled in the stone hearth despite no visible fuel source, casting warmth that carried the scent of ancient cedar and preserved memory.

"This is yours?" Caelin explored the space with growing wonder, noting weapons hung with ceremonial care beside delicate astronomical instruments.

"It was," Lucan said, uncertainty coloring his voice. "Before I died defending the undefendable."

***

He moved to light oil lamps, each flame strengthening his outline as though light itself reinforced his tenuous existence. The shadows retreated reluctantly, clinging to his edges as if they sought to reclaim him.

"Sometimes I think the city itself keeps certain places safe," he added, "holding them in trust until their owners remember how to return home."

A desk in the corner caught her attention, covered with papers bearing detailed glyph sequences she almost recognized. Different hands had written notes in margins, as though multiple scholars had worked across various time periods.

"You were studying something specific," she observed, tracing one particularly intricate diagram. The paper warmed beneath her touch, the ink brightening as though responding to contact. "Protection methods?"

"Ways to shield those I loved from divine retribution." He settled into a chair near the fire, the movement carrying a weariness that spoke of burdens carried too long. "I suspected someone had noticed our relationship and that consequences would follow."

As he spoke, the surrounding shadows deepened, gathering at his feet like pooling ink. His hands occasionally showed glimpses of the chair arms beneath them when firelight struck at certain angles.

"Did you know what would happen when we chose each other?" she asked, the soulmark pulsing beneath her shirt in rhythm with the words.

"I knew it was forbidden," he said with devastating simplicity. "I knew the traditional price for mortal love of divinity was death. For divinity returning such love, the punishment was complete erasure." His smile held edges sharp enough to cut. "I researched alternatives. Obviously, my preparations proved inadequate."

The fire popped and settled, sending sparks up the chimney. Caelin studied his face in the flickering light, noting how the shadows carved his features into something caught between human beauty and otherworldly endurance.

"Tell me about us," she said, settling into the chair across from him. "Not the cosmic implications or heaven's rules. Tell me how we started. How we found each other."

"I was assigned to Archives Guard duty when you came to walk among mortals," he began, his voice carrying the careful reverence of someone handling treasured relics. "It was considered a tremendous honor to be appointed as personal guardian to a seraph conducting research on memory preservation."

"But?"

"You started asking me questions." The memory brought warmth to his features, years of accumulated sorrow lifting. His form solidified slightly, edges becoming more defined as he connected with the memory. "About the books I read during watch shifts. About mortal poetry. You wanted to understand how humans processed concepts like grief and loss and hope, not as abstract principles but as lived experiences."

Heat stirred beneath her shirt where the soulmark rested, responding to something in his voice that bypassed rational thought entirely. She could almost see it, sitting together in some forgotten corner of the Archives's halls, heads bent over volumes of mortal verse while divine protocol collapsed under genuine curiosity.

"You were supposed to observe from distance," Lucan continued, his gaze growing distant. "Instead, you wanted to learn. You asked if I would teach you to read human poetry, help you understand how mortals found beauty in temporary things, in love that would inevitably end with death."

"Had you ever loved anyone before?" The question emerged before she could consider its implications.

"Never," he replied without hesitation. "Guardians take oaths of service that preclude personal attachments. We exist to protect and witness, not to desire or claim." He paused, studying her face. "And Elowen? Had she ever experienced what mortals call love?"

"I don't think so." The answer rose from some deep place in her consciousness, certain as sunrise. "Divine beings perceive fondness, appreciation, and even profound care for mortal existence. But love of the kind that reshapes everything you thought you understood about yourself..." She shook her head. "That was revolutionary."

The memory surfaced without warning, clear as winter starlight.

"The night you found me crying in the Archives," she whispered as the scene unfolded behind her eyes. "I'd been reading mortal accounts of loss, poetry written by those who'd watched loved ones die. I was trying to understand why humans mourned temporary things rather than celebrating their brief existence."

"You were sitting on the floor between the oldest shelves," Lucan said, his own voice rough with memory. His form grew more solid as the shared recollection strengthened their connection. "Surrounded by books and scrolls, tears falling onto pages. When I offered my cloak because divine beings grow cold when experiencing mortal emotions too deeply, you looked up at me and asked—"

"Why do mortals choose love when they know it will end?" Caelin interrupted, the words torn from her throat by a returned memory. "Why risk such pain for something that can't possibly last?"

"And I said..."

"Because some things are worth breaking for," she whispered, understanding blooming like wildfire in her chest. "Even when the breaking destroys everything we thought we were."

"That was the moment," Lucan confirmed, leaning forward until only firelight lay between them, "when I realized I would choose your safety over any oath I'd taken, your happiness over heavenly law."

"And I saw my divine nature crack open," Caelin said, hand pressing against her soulmark, where heat pulsed with increasing intensity. "Something more dangerous than duty flooding in to fill the spaces that had only held cosmic principle before."

The air between them hummed with memory and recognition. Gravity that transcended physical law drew Caelin forward, pulled by the connection that had survived death and erasure.

"I don't remember loving you," she said, honesty cutting deep between them. "But I remember being loved. Being seen and chosen as though my existence justified every risk, every consequence, every rule that had to be broken."

"You were the center of my universe," he said, absolute conviction ringing in every word. "You still are."

The statement landed like a physical blow. But close behind that recognition came uncertainty, sharp as a blade between ribs.

"How can I trust these feelings?" The question burst from her. "How do I distinguish between genuine attraction and mystical compulsion from a bond I never chose to create?"

The doubt hit the air between them like a physical force. Lucan gasped, his form flickering violently. Color drained from his features with terrifying speed, and for a horrifying moment, she could see through his chest to the chair back, his material form becoming translucent as old glass.

"Lucan!" She threw herself from her chair without conscious thought, landing on her knees beside him as he grimaced with the effort of maintaining coherence. His edges dissolved into mist, shoulders becoming indistinct, fingers fading to transparency.

"Your uncertainty," he managed, voice strained to breaking. "It weakens the connection. Breaks the threads holding me together."

Terror clawed at her chest as she watched him become increasingly translucent, his form wavering like a heat mirage. She could actually see the fire through his torso, flames distorted by flesh that couldn't decide whether it existed. Without hesitation, she reached for him with desperate hands, grasping for fingers that tried to vanish like smoke.

The moment their skin connected substance flowed back through him like ink spreading across fabric. The dangerous transparency faded from his center outward, color returning to his features, his habitual breathing deepening from ragged gasping to something approaching natural rhythm.

"You're solid again," she breathed, studying his face for signs of permanent damage. Her hands remained clasped around his, unwilling to break the contact that anchored him to existence.

"For now." His hands closed around hers with the desperation of someone who'd glimpsed the abyss. "But, Caelin, if you can't accept what we are, can't trust the connection between us—"

"I'll lose you entirely," she finished, reality settling into her bones like winter cold. "Not just to death this time but to complete unmaking."

His golden-ringed eye dimmed momentarily. "I won't pressure you into accepting feelings you can't trust," he said, though the words clearly cost him tremendous effort. "If doubt is honest, if the connection appears forced or artificial—"

"It doesn't feel false," she interrupted, surprised by the vehemence in her own voice. "It feels like coming home to a place I didn't know I'd been missing my entire life." Her thumbs brushed across his knuckles, marveled at how solid he became under her deliberate touch. "The problem isn't the feelings themselves. The problem is trusting myself to distinguish between echo and active choice."

He studied her face in the firelight, reading something that made hope bloom carefully in his features. "Then don't distinguish between them," he said, voice roughening with possibility. "Don't analyze or categorize. Just..."

His eyes found hers, one brown as rich earth, one marked with divine fire.

"Just choose. Here, now, with the knowledge and feelings you carry in this moment."

The request hung between them like an offered threshold. Caelin stared into his face, reading centuries of patient devotion in features that carried both mortal vulnerability and other-worldly endurance. He'd died defending her, waited through dissolution and resurrection, and existed in the space between life and death, powered by nothing but faith in their bond.

What did she want?

She wanted to stop questioning every instinct that drew her to him. Cease analyzing every moment of connection for signs of manipulation. Quit protecting herself from feelings that might consume her if allowed to grow to their full strength.

She wanted to choose without fear.

Her soulmark blazed beneath her shirt, matching the answering light in his marked eye.

"I choose you," she said, decision solidifying even as the words formed. "Not because I remember loving you as Elowen, but because I can see who you are now." Her voice strengthened with each word. "Someone faithful enough to wait centuries for a woman who might never remember him. A man who researched protection methods instead of fleeing when love became dangerous. One who clawed his way back from death because some bonds refuse to acknowledge endings."

His breath caught, an unnecessary but achingly human response to words that hit him like a benediction.

"I choose this," she continued, leaning closer until she felt the warmth radiating from his increasingly solid form. "Whatever we were, whatever we became, whatever we're still becoming."

The soulmarks erupted to life between them, hers beneath her shirt, his beneath worn leather, both pulsing in perfect synchrony. Violet-gold light filled the air, and for a breathless moment, the room resonated with sounds that belonged to no earthly realm, the whisper of wind through wings that weren't there, the harmonics of vows that pre-dated mortal speech.

Lucan's form solidified completely, matter flowing back through him until he appeared fully human in the firelight. More than appearance, she could see life stirring within him, responding to her acceptance with something that tran-scended mere existence.

"When you choose me without reservation," he said, won-der bleeding through his voice, "I can feel my heart trying to remember how to beat. Trying to reclaim the rhythm of actual life instead of just echoing its shadow."

"Show me," she whispered, moving closer until their knees touched. "Show me the difference choosing makes."

His hand moved to cover his soulmark that blazed beneath ancient leather. "Here. Place your hand here and learn what acceptance creates between us."

She pressed her palm flat against his chest. The moment their soulmarks aligned through fabric and skin sensation exploded between them like lightning finding ground, the phantom stirring of a heart learning to beat, lungs remembering their essential purpose, and blood moving with intention rather than habit.

"I can feel it," she breathed, wonder flooding her chest. "Your heart. It's actually trying to live again."

"Only when you touch me with purpose instead of hesitation," he admitted, covering her hand with both of his own. "Only when you choose connection rather than question it."

They sat in the firelight's warmth. Her hand pressed to his chest where life stuttered back toward true rhythm, his hands covering hers as if she was the most precious thing in any realm. The connection hummed between them, deeper than attraction, more complex than memory, two souls recognizing each other across distances that should have been unbridgeable.

A sharp knock at the door shattered the moment's perfect intimacy. Caelin jerked back instinctively, immediately missing the blazing warmth of the connection as cold air rushed between them.

***

Jalen's hands trembled as he read the instructions again, the official seal of the Order glowing with subtle power at the document's base.

SUBJECT: ELOWEN RECLAMATION PRIORITY: IMMEDIATE CONTAINMENT PROTOCOL: ALPHA-NINE

*Monitor C. Wenriel has displayed Class-4 Resonance signatures consistent with divine reawakening. Subject has accessed the Ashwell. Divine sibling Nerien has confirmed willingness to complete original erasure protocol. Your duty is to confirm subject location and maintain surveillance until the extraction team arrives.* Do not engage. *Comply immediately or face equivalent consequences.*

Sweat beaded on his forehead as he weighed years of loyalty against months of watching Caelin approach mysteries with wonder instead of fear. The Order had raised him since childhood, taught him everything he knew about preservation and protection. Their mission had always seemed righteous, maintain the barriers, protect humanity from divine caprice.

Yet in Caelin he'd seen something the Order's teachings hadn't prepared him for: divinity that enhanced humanity rather than diminished it. Power wielded with curiosity instead of dominance.

On his desk lay his meticulous notes documenting her growing abilities, evidence he should have submitted weeks ago. Instead, he'd been selectively editing his reports, emphasizing scholarly aptitude while downplaying the increasingly obvious signs of divine awakening.

"They'll erase everything she is," he whispered to the empty room. The thought of Caelin, brilliant, compassionate Caelin, being hollowed out and refilled with fabricated memories made his stomach turn. "Not just the divine parts. Everything."

His hands moved to the drawer where he kept his most dangerous discovery, ancient texts describing the Underspire and the Deeping Gate. Knowledge explicitly forbidden by the Order, sanctuary for those hunted by divine law.

Decision crystallized like ice forming in still water. He gathered his notes, the forbidden texts, and slipped the resonance tracker into his pocket. If he was going to betray everything he'd sworn to uphold, he would do it thoroughly.

The Order would come for him too once they realized what he'd done. There would be no return from this betrayal.

"So be it," he murmured, fingers tracing the outline of the resonance tracker that would lead him to Caelin and her guardian. Whatever consequences awaited, they couldn't possibly outweigh the cost of remaining silent while someone he respected was unmade.

***

"Lucan?" Jalen's voice called through the heavy wood with urgent desperation. "Are you in there? And Caelin, if you're with him, I need to speak with both of you immediately! They're coming!"

"Jalen?" Caelin stood, confusion and growing alarm replacing the peace that had settled over her. "How did he find this place?"

Lucan rose as well, his form remaining solid despite the interruption, though wariness crept into his expression. "The wards should have prevented casual discovery. Unless..."

"Unless what?"

"He carries something that resonates with divine energy. Something that would guide him to places where power accumulates." He moved toward the door with predatory caution, hand instinctively moving to where a sword should hang. "What has your friend been researching lately?"

"Memory-binding techniques," Caelin said, as ice formed in her stomach and implication dawned. "And artifacts that respond to bloodlines with unusual glyph sensitivity." Her voice dropped. "And preservation methods for divine script that most scholars consider purely theoretical."

Lucan's marked eye blazed with sudden alarm. "Caelin, exactly how much does Jalen know about your unusual reactions to restoration work? About glyphs responding to your touch in ways they don't for other preservationists?"

"Everything," she whispered, understanding crashing over her. "Every anomaly, every breakthrough, every strange occurrence. I documented all of it, shared my theories with him, and asked for his input on the most puzzling phenomena."

"Please!" Jalen's voice came again, more insistent. "I know you're both in there, the resonance signatures are unmistakable. I've discovered who's been monitoring your progress, who sent me to watch you. The Order of Preservation knows about the soulmark now! They're mobilizing tonight!"

Caelin and Lucan exchanged a look heavy with understanding and mounting dread. If Jalen had been tracking her abilities, documenting her responses to ancient glyphs, and researching bloodlines connected to pre-Collapse divinity...

"He's not just an interested colleague," Lucan said, his voice carrying the flat certainty of someone whose worst suspicions were being confirmed. "Someone assigned him to watch you. The Order of Preservation has been gathering intelligence about your awakening abilities since you first showed unusual sensitivity to the glyphs."

Footsteps circled the building urgently, and Jalen's voice dropped to a desperate whisper. "They know you went to the Ashwell. They're sending an extraction team. I was supposed to report your location, but I can't." His voice broke. "Please, we have little time."

The soulmarks pulsed between them with shared understanding. Lucan's hand found Caelin's, their fingers intertwining with purpose rather than hesitation. His form solidified further at her touch, the shadows retreating entirely as his presence became fully anchored to the physical realm.

"Whatever game is being played," he said quietly, "we face it as one."

Caelin nodded, the heat of her soulmark pulsing with new-found clarity. "As equals. By choice."

Outside, Jalen's frantic movements continued and, somewhere in the distance, the faint sound of multiple footsteps approached, measured, coordinated, and entirely too purposeful.

The battle for their right to exist had begun.

# Chapter 9

# The Deeping Gate

The silence stretched taut as a bowstring, ready to snap.

Caelin paused, hand on the ancient wood of the door's handle. She could feel Lucan's presence behind her, his warmth and solidity a comfort in the face of mounting uncertainty. Their connection, the one that had only just stabilized minutes before, hummed between them like a current, strengthening her resolve. Jalen's voice continued to plead from outside, but she couldn't bring herself to open the door just yet.

"Caelin, I know how this appears, but you have to listen," Jalen's voice cracked, desperation stripping away his scholarly composure. "The resonance signatures are strengthening, they're almost here. Minutes, not hours."

"Resonance signatures," Lucan growled, moving closer to Caelin. His form remained solid, but tension radiated from him in waves. "That's not terminology an ordinary preservationist would use."

Through the heavy wood, they heard Jalen's sharp intake of breath, the sound of someone realizing their careful deceptions had just crumbled to ash. When he spoke again, defeat weighted every word.

"I'm not a typical preservationist," Jalen admitted, his voice dropping to barely above a whisper. "Please, let me explain before you decide I'm another threat to eliminate."

Caelin examined the door intently, tracing the ancient protective glyphs carved into its surface. Her instincts warred within her, the scholarly caution that had defined Caelin Wenriel battling against the awakening divine intuition of Elowen. Should she trust the eager scholar who had been nothing but supportive, or protect the revenant whose life literally depended on her belief?

"If I open that door and he betrays us," she said quietly, "the shock could unravel your connection entirely. I've seen how doubt affects your coherence."

Lucan's hand found hers, fingers intertwining with the fluid certainty of long practice. His touch remained warm and reassuringly solid, the bond between them having strengthened during their earlier conversation.

"But failure to heed his warning about actual threats might cost us our sole opportunity to outmaneuver whatever forces are closing in," he countered, his marked eye pulsing with subtle golden light. "I can feel something pressing against the outer wards already."

The weight of decision settled across her shoulders like wings she'd forgotten how to use. Fear wrestled with intuition and caution grappled with the growing divine awareness that whispered of time running out.

"Your choice," Lucan added, voice gentling. "But make it quickly."

Caelin turned the lock with deliberate precision, opening the door just wide enough to see Jalen's face. He stumbled into the room, eyes wide with a mixture of terror and determination. Ink stained his shirt and his sandy hair was disheveled from what looked like frantic pacing. It was his eyes that held her attention, bright with fear and hope, as he took in their proximity and the visible energy shimmering between them.

"Thank every power that watches over impossible things," he breathed, sagging against the doorframe. "When the divine resonance spiked and then suddenly stabilized..." His gaze moved between them, taking in details that shouldn't have been visible to ordinary perception. "You've sealed the preliminary bond. I can actually see the energy flowing between your soulmarks."

Lucan stepped protectively between Jalen and Caelin, his shadow solidifying beneath him, a subtle but important sign that their connection remained strong despite this intrusion. "Explain how you recognize divine resonance. How you identify sealed bonds that shouldn't exist in any normal scholar's experience."

Jalen swallowed hard, setting his satchel down with hands that trembled. He glanced toward the windows, then back at them, fear sharpening his movements.

"Because monitoring such phenomena has been my assignment from the beginning," he admitted, words tumbling out in a rush. "I was placed in the Preservation Society to document Caelin's developing abilities, catalog every anomaly, and track every sign that her divine nature might reassert itself."

The betrayal hit Caelin like a physical blow. Her soulmark flared beneath her clothing, violet light bleeding through the fabric as anger ignited within her.

"You've been spying on me." Her voice dropped dangerously low. "Every conversation, every shared discovery, every moment I thought I was working with someone who understood—"

"Was genuine," Jalen interrupted, stepping forward despite Lucan's warning glare. "The friendship was real, Caelin. The admiration for your insights, the excitement over your breakthroughs, all of that was completely honest." His hands trembled as he reached for his satchel. "And that's why I'm here now, breaking every oath I've taken, because I can't stand by and let them erase you again."

"Then why?" The question emerged harsh with accumulated pain. "Why the surveillance? Why the deception?"

"Because I work for people who believe fallen divinity should remain fallen." His admission came out just above a whisper. "The Order of Preservation. They've existed since the Collapse, dedicated to maintaining the barriers between mortal and celestial realms."

The name struck a chord in Caelin's memory, something she'd glimpsed in ancient texts during restoration work but dismissed as scholarly speculation. Now those fragments connected, forming a pattern too deliberate to be coincidence.

"I remember references to them," she said, the scholar in her momentarily overriding betrayal. "Guardians of the veil between realms, protectors against divine interference."

"More than that," Lucan added, his expression darkening. "They're the ones who helped implement your erasure after the Collapse. The mortal arm of divine justice."

Jalen nodded, reluctant confirmation written across his features. "They've monitored Elowen's Fall for centuries, watching for signs of your reemergence. When you began working with artifacts that responded unusually to your touch—"

"They sent you," Caelin finished, the pieces clicking into terrible alignment. "To determine whether I was merely gifted or something more dangerous."

***

"Which conclusion did you reach?" Lucan demanded, his form growing more solid as Caelin's rising power strengthened their connection.

"She's absolutely the most dangerous being walking any realm," Jalen said without hesitation. "She's remembering not just personal history but cosmic truths that were buried for excellent reasons. And if she reclaims her divine nature, the established order of reality could change in ways that make the original Collapse look like a minor disruption."

The room fell silent except for the crackling of the fire. Caelin felt Lucan's presence as an anchor, his steady warmth the only thing keeping divine fury from overwhelming mortal restraint.

"But you didn't report those conclusions," Lucan observed, reading implications in Jalen's confession.

"I couldn't." Jalen's shoulders slumped. "Because somewhere in those months of working beside her, watching her approach every puzzle with wonder instead of fear, I realized something that changed everything." He looked directly at Caelin, eyes bright with conviction. "I realized some kinds of power exist because they're supposed to, regardless of how much they upset comfortable certainties."

A sharp crack split the air as one of the outer wards shattered. The building trembled, ancient wood groaning as protective symbols flared around the perimeter.

"They're coming," Jalen said, urgency replacing reflection. He reached into his satchel, withdrawing a scroll that seemed to absorb light rather than reflect it. The text on its surface constantly shifted, preventing any stable meaning from forming. "Divine binding contracts authored by entities predating written law. Erasure wards capable of removing beings from the fundamental fabric of existence itself."

From outside came a sound that made Caelin's blood freeze. It was deliberate chanting in a language not meant for human tongues.Each syllable seemed to bend reality around it, creating pockets of wrongness in the air. Through the window, she glimpsed hooded figures in ash gray robes forming a precise circle around the building. They moved with unnatural synchronicity, each raising a crystalline rod that hummed with suppressive energy.

The temperature plummeted as though winter itself had been invited through the windows. Frost began forming on glass despite the fire's warmth.

"Order Enforcers," Jalen whispered, fear rendering his voice almost inaudible. "They're using nullification artifacts, tools specifically designed to bind divine essence and prevent its expression."

The chanting intensified, and a second ward shattered with the sound of breaking glass. This time, the magical backlash was visible, a ripple of blue-white energy that collapsed inward, leaving a hole in the protective barrier surrounding them.

Through this breach, one of the crystalline rods flew with impossible precision, embedding itself in the floor at Lucan's feet. A pulse of sickly white energy erupted from it, washing over him in concentric waves. The effect was immediate and horrifying. Where the energy touched his form unraveled at the edges, becoming translucent and unstable.

Lucan dropped to one knee with a strangled cry, his eye dimming as his connection to Caelin temporarily destabilized. "Containment rod," he gasped, trying to maintain coherence. "Designed to...disrupt the bond...between divinity and its anchors."

"And they've established contact with the one who erased you originally," Jalen continued, clearly reluctant to reveal this last detail as he helped Caelin pull Lucan away from the artifact's influence. "Your divine sibling has agreed to complete what they began centuries ago."

"Nerien," Caelin whispered, the name sending tremors through reality itself. The soulmark beneath her collarbone blazed with such intensity that violet light illuminated the room, casting eerie shadows across ancient walls.

Memory surfaced, a face like her own yet not, shimmering with silver light instead of violet, eyes filled with terrible purpose as judgment descended. Not hatred but something worse: the absolute conviction that love must be sacrificed for cosmic order.

***

Through the window, she saw one of the Order members step forward, lowering her hood to reveal severe features framed by silver-streaked hair. The woman held up an artifact that resembled a compass, its needle spinning frantically before locking directly on Caelin. Their eyes met across the distance, and recognition flashed between them.

"Magistra Levain," Caelin breathed, shock adding fresh betrayal to the moment. The stern woman who had sponsored her research grant and who had provided access to restricted archives for her restoration work. "She's one of them."

"Senior Enforcer Levain," Jalen corrected grimly. "She's been monitoring you since your university days, tracking every sign of awakening."

Levain raised her hand and the chanting shifted to a higher, more urgent cadence. The remaining wards flickered, weakening under the coordinated assault.

"How long do we have?" Lucan asked, struggling to his feet as Caelin's proximity helped stabilize his form. He moved toward cabinets that held weapons and traveling supplies, each step more solid than the last.

"Not long," Jalen replied, glancing nervously at the windows where frost patterns grew more complex by the second. "Divine beings of such magnitude require preparation for manifestation in mortal realms, but the Order has been facilitating this for days. They only sped up their timeline when they detected your bond stabilizing."

Through the window, Caelin watched in horror as the Order members each produced a small silver bowl. In perfect unison, they cut their palms, allowing blood to flow into the vessels. As the blood pooled, it glowed with the same silver light she associated with Nerien's power. Mortal essence willingly sacrificed to create anchor points for divine manifestation.

"Blood anchors," Lucan hissed, recognizing the ritual. "They're creating a summoning circle that will allow Nerien to manifest without the usual constraints. They're literally cutting holes in reality's fabric."

Jalen pulled out another scroll, this one covered with his own frantic handwriting in multiple inks, additions made in obvious haste. "But I found something in the restricted archives, references that weren't supposed to survive the systematic purges after the Collapse." His scholar's excitement briefly overcame fear. "The Underspire, beneath our city's oldest foundations. And something called the Deeping Gate."

Lucan went still, the preternatural stillness of a predator assessing a lethal threat. "Where exactly did you encounter those terms?"

"Records sealed in the deepest Archives's vaults, fragmentary references in texts marked for destruction." Jalen spread the scroll on a nearby table, revealing diagrams of the city's underground structure. "They speak of a threshold that recognizes divine essence, a gateway that opens only to those carrying sufficient power to survive what lies beyond."

"We need to leave," Lucan said, retrieving a sword whose leather wrapping bore the smooth wear of centuries of use. The blade gleamed with an inner light as he unsheathed it briefly, checking its edge. "If Nerien is truly manifesting..." He stopped midmotion, something in his expression shifting to alarm. "The Deeping Gate. Caelin, that's not sanctuary. That's judgment."

"What do you mean?" she demanded, watching him buckle the blade at his hip with movements that spoke of muscle memory older than his apparent age.

"It's a test that determines whether you're strong enough to reclaim what they took from you," he replied, his voice dropping to a whisper, as though the very walls might be listening. "Or whether attempting such a reclamation will destroy everything you've become in the interim."

Another rod crashed through the window, landing closer to Caelin this time. The pulse of energy it released made her soulmark burn with painful intensity, as though something was trying to sever the connection from within. Outside, Levain's voice rose above the others, calling out words that seemed to bend around corners of reality never meant to be touched.

"Elowen-that-was, by authority vested in the Order of Preservation and the Cosmic Accord, your essence is claimed for nullification and redistribution. Your memories will be purged, your divine spark extinguished, and your mortal vessel cleansed of celestial influence."

Each word carried weight beyond mere sound, reality itself seeming to bend toward Levain as though acknowledging her authority. The room's temperature dropped further, frost creeping across the floor in intricate patterns that resembled binding sigils.

"We go now," Lucan decided, moving toward a section of wall that revealed itself as a concealed doorway when he pressed against a specific glyph. Ancient stone ground against stone as the passage opened. "Before the Order completes their preparations and Nerien arrives with full divine authority."

He glanced back at Jalen, his expression caught between gratitude and lingering mistrust. "You're welcome to accompany us if conscience demands it but understand, where we're going, scholarly observation becomes impossible. The Deeping Gate changes those who approach it."

Jalen shouldered his satchel without hesitation. "I've spent months documenting impossible phenomena. I believe I can handle some personal transformation."

"Assume nothing," Lucan warned, leading them into passages that descended through foundations older than recorded history. "The Gate doesn't just test divine nature. It reveals truth without mercy or comfort, strips away every illusion we use to make existence tolerable."

The crash of the building's main door being breached echoed down the passage behind them. Footsteps pounded on ancient wood, accompanied by the crystalline hum of nullification rods and the continued chanting that seemed to bend space itself.

"They've breached the inner sanctum," Jalen gasped, hurrying forward. "The Order's Enforcers are trained to track divine resonance through any barrier, physical or metaphysical."

As they moved deeper, Caelin felt the bond between her and Lucan strengthening further, as though the ancient stone itself amplified their connection. She reached for his hand in the darkness, unerringly finding it despite the minimal light from phosphorescent moss clinging to the damp walls.

"How did you know about these tunnels?" she asked as they navigated increasingly narrow passages.

"I helped build them," Lucan replied, his voice echoing strangely in the confined space. "After we realized our bond might draw unwanted attention, I created escape routes throughout the city. Some knowledge survives even death and rebirth."

***

Behind them, a ripple of energy pulsed through the tunnel, distorting the air like heat waves above the summer stone. The Order's nullification magic was seeping into the passages, seeking a divine essence to bind and contain.

"They're tracking us through the bond itself," Lucan warned, pulling Caelin faster. "Our connection leaves traces they can follow."

The tunnels grew more ancient as they descended, walls lined with glyphs that pulsed with their own illumination. Some Caelin recognized from restoration work but others belonged to scripts that predated mortal language entirely. The air thickened with accumulated power, each breath requiring deliberate effort as though the atmosphere itself had weight.

A shout echoed from behind, too close, much too close. The unmistakable sound of boots on stone and the metallic clatter of specialized equipment. Caelin glanced back to see bobbing lights in the darkness, the silver glow of nullification rods illuminating the gray-robed figures in pursuit.

"There!" came Levain's voice, sharp with authority. "The divine signature is strongest in that direction. Deploy containment measures!"

A whistling sound cut through the air as something long and slender flew past Caelin's ear, embedding itself in the tunnel wall ahead. Another rod, this one different, longer, with glyphs etched along its length that glowed with hungry purpose.

"Boundary stake," Jalen gasped. "They're setting up a containment perimeter. If they complete the circle..."

"We'll be trapped in a pocket of nullified space," Lucan finished, drawing his sword. The blade's glow intensified in response to the threat, golden light spilling from ancient metal to illuminate their path. "Run. Don't look back."

Another stake whistled past, then another. Each one that found purchase in stone emitted a high, keening note that seemed to slice through divine energy like a blade. Caelin felt each one as a physical pressure against her awakening power, like hands trying to force her back into a smaller shape.

"How much farther?" Jalen asked, his scholarly composure cracking as the walls seemed to press closer and the sounds of pursuit grew louder.

"Distance becomes negotiable near thresholds between realms," Lucan replied, his marked eye gleaming brighter in the darkness. "We're not traveling through normal space anymore."

The tunnel ahead forked, and Lucan pulled them sharply left without hesitation. The passage narrowed further, forcing them to move single file through spaces that seemed barely wide enough to accommodate their bodies. Behind them, the Order members slowed, forced to navigate the constricting tunnel with their bulky equipment.

"They can't follow as quickly here," Jalen observed, panting. "These passages weren't designed for people carrying nullification gear."

"They weren't designed for people at all," Lucan said grimly. "These are the paths divine essence travels between realms. We're following routes that exist between states of being not physical locations."

As if summoned by his words, the tunnels they traversed abruptly widened, opening into a chamber that defied comprehension. Vaulted ceilings soared overhead, stone glowing with an inner light that cast no shadows. At the chamber's far end rose the Deeping Gate, an arch formed from a living rock that shifted between deep blue and midnight black, veins of silver pulsing like a heartbeat.

Standing before it, motionless as a carved monument, was a figure in ash gray robes.

***

The Watcher turned as they approached, movement so fluid it seemed less human motion than shadow given form. No features were visible beneath their deep hood, but something about their bearing struck Caelin as hauntingly familiar, a presence that resonated with her awakening divine senses.

When they spoke, their voice carried harmonics that echoed from the chamber itself, as though the stone amplified words that originated beyond mortal comprehension.

"Three approach where only one may enter. Three carry burdens, but only one bears the choice that reshapes worlds."

"Who are you?" Caelin demanded, though something about the figure tugged at memories hovering just beyond reach.

"I am what endures when duty outlasts the one who bore it," the Watcher replied, attention fixing on her with an intensity that made her soulmark blaze in immediate response. "What lingers when love proves stronger than death but not quite strong enough for complete victory."

Caelin felt Lucan tense beside her, his grip on her hand tightening almost imperceptibly. Something in the Watcher's voice affected him deeply, recognition struggling against confusion.

From the tunnel behind them came the sounds of pursuit, closer now, the Order having navigated the narrow passages. Silver light spilled into the chamber as the first of the Enforcers emerged, Levain at their head. She raised a hand, and three of her subordinates immediately deployed into a triangular formation, each planting a boundary stake that hummed with containment energy.

"The Deeping Gate opens only to those willing to surrender everything they believe themselves to be," the Watcher continued, voice carrying warnings that echoed with prophetic weight, seemingly undisturbed by the intrusion. "Those who enter must face truth without illusion's comfort, memory without time's merciful buffer, and choice without ignorance's protective veil."

"Surrender the divine remnant," Levain commanded, her voice carrying the weight of centuries of Order authority. "The entity you harbor is not yours to protect, nor is its power yours to wield."

The chamber's air grew dense with competing forces. The Watcher's ancient authority, the Order's nullification energy, Caelin's awakening divinity, and the Gate's hungry power all converged in a maelstrom of potential.

"What lies beyond the Gate?" Jalen asked, scholarly curiosity overcoming obvious terror as he positioned himself between the Order members and Caelin.

"The Underspire," the Watcher replied without shifting attention from Caelin. "Where choice's roots grow deep enough to reshape reality's foundations. Where broken things can be mended, lost ones reclaimed, and forbidden things made lawful through a will strong enough to rewrite existence."

"And if someone isn't strong enough?" Caelin asked, though dread curled in her stomach.

"Then the Gate becomes a tomb, and the Underspire claims another soul too weak to bear absolute truth's weight." The Watcher stepped aside with ceremonial precision, revealing the entrance in all its terrifying completeness. "Choose quickly, daughter of memory and flame. Those who would unmake you draw closer with each heartbeat, and some thresholds open only once."

Levain barked an order, and the Order members advanced, forming a half circle of containment energy that pushed toward Caelin with inexorable purpose. Each rod they carried emitted pulses of energy that made Lucan's form waver at the edges. His connection to physical reality was temporarily disrupted.

"Now, Elowen-that-was," Levain intoned, her voice dropping into registers that resonated with the chamber itself. "Your sibling comes to complete what was begun. Your error will be unmade, your defiance corrected, and cosmic law restored."

The darkness within the arch pulsed with hypnotic rhythm, calling to something deep in Caelin's divine nature while simultaneously warning her mortal consciousness that what lay beyond could destroy everything she'd built in this carefully constructed lifetime.

Behind them, the sound of silver bells grew louder, accompanied by temperature drops that made their breath visible in the increasingly frigid air. Reality itself seemed to thin, creating space for something vast to manifest.

Caelin stared into the Gate's hungry darkness. Destiny solidified around her like ice forming on still water. Forward into an unknown truth that might destroy her, or backward into assured erasure that definitely would?

She took a step toward the threshold, feeling reality bend around her decision.

The Watcher inclined their head in what might have been approval. "Enter, and discover whether love's power surpasses that of law, or if law's strength will prevail over hearts defying cosmic order."

The Gate's darkness pulsed once, twice, like a heart remembering how to beat.

Levain raised her hands, and the Order members each activated their containment rods in perfect synchrony. A web of silvery energy formed between them, reaching toward Caelin with tendrils that promised painless but complete annihilation.

Behind them came a voice that shattered the chamber's stillness, clear and resonant with power that made the very stone tremble in recognition: "Sister mine, your running ends here."

Caelin turned to see silver light bleeding into the chamber, casting no shadows but illuminating everything with merciless clarity. Nerien hadn't fully manifested yet, but their presence pressed against reality like a storm gathering strength. Where this divine light touched the Order members, they dropped to their knees in reverence, their nullification tools suddenly crude and inadequate before true celestial power.

She looked back at Lucan, drinking in every detail as though she might never see him again. The sharp line of his jaw caught the chamber's ethereal light, and his dark hair fell across his forehead in a way that made her fingers ache to brush it back. One eye held the warm brown of rich earth, familiar and grounding, while the other burned with that pale ring of golden fire, divine judgment made into something beautiful by the devotion blazing in both. Even now, as fear flickered across his features, he watched her with careful reverence, as though she was something precious rather than dangerous.

Their soulmarks pulsed in perfect synchrony, violet and gold light merging where they stood close. She could feel their connection humming between them, stronger than it had been since her awakening began.

"If I don't return..." she began, throat tightening around words that refused to form.

"You will," the Watcher said with absolute certainty. "Or you will become something that makes return irrelevant."

The air turned knife-sharp with cold, an overwhelming hum filling the space, a resonance that warped reality itself, making room for an immense presence about to manifest. The silver light intensified, no longer merely illuminating but transforming, reshaping the chamber to accommodate divine manifestation.

Heart pounding, Caelin sprinted forward. She dove into the Gate's ravenous void just as blinding silver light erupted behind her, Nerien's form igniting the room with the intensity of a supernova. The echo of Lucan's voice reached her ears, calling her name with desperate urgency and unwavering belief.

"I'll find you!" His promise cut through the chaos, the last thing she heard before darkness consumed everything.

The Deeping Gate sealed shut with finality, like skin knitting over a fresh wound, severing her from the world she'd known and thrusting her toward truths she wasn't certain she could survive.

# CHAPTER 10
# THE SILVER ROOT

T he darkness breathed.

Caelin opened her eyes to walls that pulsed with veins of silver light, each throb synchronized with the rhythm beneath her ribs. This wasn't the familiar stone of Elowen's Fall or the comforting weight of earth above her head. The chamber stretched impossibly wide, its ceiling lost in shadows that moved like living silk, while beneath her feet the floor felt warm and alive.

She pushed herself upright, muscles trembling with the aftershock of crossing the Deeping Gate. Her fingertips tingled where she'd touched stone that wasn't quite stone, and the air carried scents that had no earthly source, ozone and starlight, a memory made physical.

The Underspire. The name surfaced in her consciousness with the weight of absolute knowledge. This place existed outside normal architecture, beyond the laws that governed mortal construction. It responded to consciousness itself, reshaping around intention and desire and the deep truths people carried in their bones.

As she stood, the walls rippled outward like water disturbed by thrown stones. Passages opened where none had existed moments before, corridors branching in directions that made her eyes water when she tried to follow them. The structure rebuilt itself around her presence, recognizing something in her that required particular navigation.

Above her, far above, she felt Lucan's presence like a dying ember in winter air. The connection strained with each moment of separation, growing thinner as his form struggled to maintain coherence without her constant choice to anchor him. That awareness sharpened her focus. She couldn't linger here indefinitely.

"The path down leads through remembering," she said to the breathing chamber. Her voice echoed strangely, each word returning changed, layered with harmonics that spoke in languages she'd never learned. Knowledge surfaced with no visible source, certain as a heartbeat. She would have to descend through layers of memory to reach whatever truth waited at this place's heart, not glimpses or fragments but complete immersion.

The silver veins in the walls brightened, forming patterns that looked almost like a script. Divine script, she realized, glyphs writing and rewriting themselves as though the Underspire spoke in the language of heaven.

A doorway opened ahead of her, outlined in a light that called to something deep in her bones. Through it, she glimpsed stairs descending into depths that glowed with their own radiance. Each step seemed carved from memory itself, solid beneath inspection but trembling with potential energy.

She stepped over the threshold.

The first chamber bloomed into existence around her, light pouring from everywhere and nowhere, warm as a summer afternoon but charged with power that raised the fine hairs on her arms. She stood in a space that existed before mortals invented architecture, where thought became structure and will shaped reality.

Then the memory seized her with the force of drowning.

*She was Elowen, and she was being born.*

Pain lanced through her temples as the divine memory collided with her mortal consciousness. Caelin gasped, falling to her knees as two identities warred within her skull. Her vision fragmented, one eye seeing the chamber, the other filled with visions of celestial birth. A high-pitched keening filled her ears, the sound of a mind trying to process what it was never designed to contain.

"Too much," she whispered, her voice layered with harmonics that didn't belong to her mortal throat. "I can't... I'm losing... "

Her fingers fumbled at her belt, closing around the small vial of Ashwell water. The cool glass against her skin provided a momentary anchor as the memory continued its assault. With trembling hands, she uncorked the vial and swallowed a careful sip. The water hit her tongue like liquid reality, cool and clarifying, drawing boundaries around her fracturing sense of self.

"I am Caelin," she murmured, the harmonics receding from her voice. "I am Caelin, who contains Elowen, not Elowen erasing Caelin."

The water's effect spread through her system, not suppressing the memory but creating a protective barrier around her consciousness. Like watching through glass instead of drowning in the tide. She could observe now, experience without dissolving.

Born not of flesh but from the primordial utterance, she emerged as light danced through her form, consciousness weaving itself from boundless potential. Her essence shimmered in vibrant violet hues. Beside her, another presence materialized, a figure of silvery grace, embodying law and order to her vivid tapestry of memory.

*Nerien.*

The name carried love so profound it hurt to contain, and recognition went deeper than thought. Not romantic love, as they were beyond mortal gender, but something fundamental, the joy of perfect completion. They were twin-forged, created as one principle split into complementary halves, designed to work in harmony so complete that neither could exist meaningfully without the other.

*Together, we are the Chorus.*

The understanding flooded through Caelin like molten gold filling a mold. They maintained the tension between divine will and mortal experience, ensuring celestial law served growth not stagnation and preserving mortal memory without letting it become a prison. She felt the weight of every soul in creation pressing against her awareness, each one precious, each one requiring careful attention.

The responsibility crushed and elevated simultaneously, the beautiful, terrible duty of caring perfectly for all of it, forever.

Her soulmark flared beneath her collarbone, burning with recognition and loss. Above her, Lucan's presence dimmed further, their connection stretching thinner with each moment of separation. The pain of that weakening bond provided an anchor to her mortal self even as divine memory threatened to overwhelm her.

Caelin staggered as the chamber dissolved like mist around her. Her mortal mind reeled under the weight of divine purpose while something deeper awakened in response, stretching like wings she'd forgotten how to use.

Another doorway beckoned, its threshold humming with different energy. She crossed it before fear could make her hesitate.

The Archives's halls stretched in graceful curves, their shelves holding the collected wisdom of mortal civilizations.

With practiced ease, Elowen moved among them, meticulously documenting and safeguarding knowledge hard-won through struggle and sacrifice, determined to prevent its loss to the relentless march of time.

*And there, standing guard beside a reading alcove, was someone who would unmake everything.*

The moment of first seeing Lucan hit Caelin with devastating precision. He stood with a guardian's disciplined posture, hand resting on his sword's hilt in the trained readiness of someone sworn to protection. But his dark eyes were fixed on an open book of mortal poetry, lips moving silently as he shaped words that carried no strategic importance, no tactical value.

"The heart builds altars where reason fears to worship," he murmured, voice barely audible but carrying such reverence that something in Elowen's celestial chest clenched with unexpected recognition.

She'd approached then, divine curiosity overcoming protocols that insisted on distance between seraph and mortal guardian. "You read mortal verse?"

"When duty permits." He'd startled at her attention but maintained respectful boundaries, though she caught the way his gaze lingered on her face as though memorizing details he had no right to notice. "Their poets see truth from angles that escape divine philosophy."

"What truth does this one capture?"

His eyes had met hers then, dark and serious and carrying depths that spoke of someone who reflected on questions with no easy answers. "Some things matter more than wisdom. Some choices are right despite every argument against them."

The conversation should have ended there. Divine beings observed and moved on. They didn't linger to discuss the philosophical implications of mortal poetry with their assigned protectors. They certainly didn't notice how thoughtfulness transformed a pleasant face into something that caught the breath and refused to let go.

But Elowen lingered. Had asked more questions. Had returned to that alcove each day, ostensibly to continue her archival work but actually to discover what new verses Lucan had found, what insights he'd gleaned from a mortal understanding of existence's beautiful complexities.

The memory faded gently, leaving Caelin with a sense of beginning. Understanding now how it had started, not with grand passion or forbidden desire, but with curiosity about someone who found beauty in temporary things and who valued truth regardless of its source.

As she prepared to descend to the third chamber, a violent spasm rocked through her body. The boundaries between Caelin and Elowen blurred without warning, her soulmark flaring with such intensity that her skin became translucent, internal organs briefly visible through flesh suddenly lighter than matter.

"No," she gasped, feeling her mortal self beginning to unravel. Memories not yet accessed flooded her awareness, centuries of existence compressed into seconds, overwhelming her mind's capacity to sort and process. Blood trickled from her nose, copper-bright on her tongue as vessels ruptured under the strain.

Her fingers, now glowing with violet light, reached again for the Ashwell water. She took another sip, larger this time, fear making her desperate. The water sizzled against her transformed flesh, steam rising from her lips as mortality and divinity negotiated their uneasy coexistence.

"Stay present," she commanded herself, pressing her palm against the wall to ground herself in physical sensation. "One memory at a time. One step at a time."

Her body gradually solidified, the painful luminescence fading from her skin. The water had bought her more time, but she could feel its effects lasting shorter amounts of time with each use. Her transformation was speeding up, mortal consciousness struggling to contain what it was never designed to hold.

Her hand pressed against her soulmark, which throbbed in response to the memory. Above her, Lucan's presence flickered dangerously, the connection between them growing more tenuous. Time was running out. The Underspire might hold answers, but it also threatened to separate them permanently if she lingered too long in its depths.

***

She descended through reality that shifted like water around her feet to the third chamber.

Weeks had passed since that first conversation. Elowen taught Lucan to read divine script by candlelight, their heads bent close together over volumes that pulsed with their own inner radiance. The air smelled of old parchment and melted wax and something indefinable that belonged only to those moments when two souls drew near enough to share the same breath.

His fingers traced glyphs with careful precision while she explained their deeper meanings, how each symbol held not just sound but intention crystallized into form. The weight of divine law made manifest in curves and lines that hummed with accumulated power.

"This one means preservation," she said, guiding his hand to a complex character. The warmth of his skin sent small shock waves through her celestial awareness. "But see how the curves fold back on themselves? It's not about keeping things unchanged. It's about holding space for growth within continuity."

"Like memory itself," he said, understanding blooming across his features as candlelight caught in his dark eyes. "We don't save the precise moment, but its core meaning. The emotion that made it worth remembering."

Wonder flooded through her at how perfectly he'd grasped what took most divine beings centuries to understand. "Yes. Exactly like that."

Their gazes met across the small space between them and something fundamental shifted. Recognition deeper than rational thought. Connection that transcended every careful boundary between mortal and divine, between guardian and guarded.

"Elowen," he said, her name carrying weight it had never held before. Not title or rank but something precious. Personal. Chosen.

"Lucan," she replied, and felt the careful walls around her celestial heart crack like ice on the lake in spring.

This memory released Caelin more gently than the others but left her sitting on stairs that shifted beneath her touch like living wood. She traced one finger along a stone that felt more like skin, understanding with growing clarity how love had grown through minor revelations rather than sudden passion. Through shared wonder and gradual recognition that some connections transcended every rule designed to prevent them.

The gentle release proved deceptive. As she stood, her vision doubled, then tripled. The Underspire multiplied around her, not one reality but dozens, each showing different versions of the same moment. In one, Elowen turned away from Lucan, choosing duty. In another, they were discovered, punishment swift and terrible. In yet another, they ascended together to some higher form of existence.

"Not real," Caelin muttered, pressing her palms against her eyes. "Just possibilities. Fragments."

But the visions persisted, growing more solid with each heartbeat. Her consciousness stretched between them like taffy pulled too thin, threatening to snap entirely. Something hot and wet ran from her ears, more blood, she realized dimly.

Her legs gave way beneath her, and she collapsed against the shifting stairs. The vial of Ashwell water tumbled from her belt, rolling precariously toward the edge of a step. With desperate focus, she lunged for it, catching the precious container before it could shatter.

Only half remained now. She had to be more careful, more measured. But as another wave of disorientation hit, bringing flashes of wings erupting from her shoulders, of skin dissolving into pure light, she knew she needed it again.

A smaller sip this time. Just enough to bring the multiple realities crashing back into one. Just enough to remember she was Caelin first, Elowen second.

The water burned going down, her transformed system fighting against its grounding properties. For a terrifying moment, it seemed to have no effect. The visions continued, her body still flickering between states of matter and energy.

Then, slowly, reality merged. The phantom wings receded. Her flesh became solid once more. But the effort left her gasping, curled around herself on stairs that pulsed with sympathy beneath her.

"I don't know if I can do this," she whispered to the surrounding emptiness. Above her, Lucan's presence dimmed further, the connection stretched to breaking. "I don't know if I can hold together long enough."

Her soulmark pulsed with fierce heat, reminding her of the weakening connection to Lucan above. Each memory integrated more of her divine self, but at what cost to her present bonds?

With an effort that felt like moving mountains, she forced herself back to her feet. One more chamber. She could endure one more memory before facing the heart of the Underspire itself.

***

The fourth chamber opened before her like a flower blooming in the space of a single heartbeat. She stepped through its threshold into paradise itself.

A hidden garden that was carpeted with violets, their purple blooms soft as silk and brightening faintly with reflected light. Ancient trees formed a natural bower overhead, their branches heavy with blossoms that smelled of honey. No mortal realm had ever contained such concentrated beauty, such a perfect sanctuary designed for a single sacred purpose.

The memory seized Caelin with an erotic intensity that stole her breath.

Elowen spread her wings in the enclosed space, violet flames streaming from each feather to illuminate the flowers below like living stars. Lucan's hands mapped the luminous contours of her divine form with reverent precision, his touch sending cascades of celestial fire through every nerve she possessed. Mortal fingers traced patterns of worship across skin that shimmered with starlight.

"I dream of you," he murmured against the hollow of her throat where power pulsed like a second heartbeat. His voice was rough with want and wonder and love so desperate it reshaped the surrounding air. "When I should think of duty, of proper distance, of maintaining the boundaries that protect us both I dream of this."

"What do you dream?" The words left her lips as prayer and invitation combined. "Tell me."

His breath caught as her wings curved around them both, creating a shelter of living light. "I dream of touching you without fear. Of seeing you not as divinity to guard but as the woman who laughs when she discovers new poetry. The one who traces glyphs with such reverence, as though each symbol contains someone's heart."

"I have never felt more divine than in the moment I allow myself to feel human," she moaned, divine ardor flowing through her at his words. "I am not just divinity. When I'm with you,

I feel like something more. Something I was meant to be but never knew existed."

"Show me." His hands stilled on her skin, dark eyes searching her face. "Show me who you are when you're not bound by celestial law."

She answered by taking his mouth with hers, pouring starlight into the kiss until he gasped against her lips. When she guided his hands to the places where celestial flames burned brightest, his touch became worship made manifest.

"You tremble," she marveled, feeling the fine vibration in his fingers as they explored the curve of her waist where energy concentrated like liquid gold.

"Because I understand what this means," he said, voice breaking with the weight of it. "Touching you like this. It's not just desire, Elowen. It's choosing you over everything I've ever been taught about what's possible, what's right, what's safe."

"And I choose you over everything I've ever known about what I am." She laid back among the violets with deliberate grace, purple petals soft as silk beneath her spreading wings, while moonlight traced silver patterns across his skin. "I choose growth over stagnation. Choice over law. Love over duty."

When his hands found the curves of her body, sacred light poured through the connection, making his eyes blaze with reflected celestial radiance. This was a transgression beyond any law. Divinity yielding to mortal touch, heaven bowing to earth's patient, devoted worship.

"Does it hurt?" he asked, pausing as her light flared brighter. "The fire?"

"No," she breathed, arching under his touch. "It feels like awakening. Like becoming real for the first time."

His lips brushed the spot on her throat where divine energy pulsated, and she groaned his name, breath hitching as ecstasy coursed through her. Her skin, radiant with celestial essence, shimmered more vividly with every tender touch. Each shared moment of closeness unraveled the very fabric of what was deemed possible between their worlds.

"I love you," he said against her skin, the words carrying the weight of vows spoken in defiance of cosmic order. "Not because you're divine. Not despite it. But because you chose to love mortal things, temporary beauty, poetry that will fade. Because you chose to love me."

"And I love you," she replied, divine fire streaming from her skin to illuminate his face like dawn breaking across mountain peaks, "because you see worth in fleeting things. Because you taught me that some choices matter more than eternity itself."

When he joined with her, violet fire and golden light burst between them to illuminate the garden like a second dawn. This was more than physical union. It was the forging of something unprecedented in all of creation's history. Two souls learning to share the same heartbeat, to breathe the same sacred air.

The erotic intensity of the memory overwhelmed Caelin's defenses completely. Her consciousness fractured, Elowen's experience becoming not memory but present reality. She was no longer observing but living it, her mortal identity submerged beneath divine ecstasy.

"I choose this," Elowen gasped as divine pleasure built to heights that threatened to consume them both, her wings spreading wide enough to shelter them from any watching eyes.

"And I choose you," Lucan replied, moving with her in perfect rhythm while celestial fire poured through them both. "Over reason, over safety, over life itself if necessary."

The moment of shared climax shattered reality itself. Caelin's consciousness blinked out entirely, her mortal mind unable to process the intensity of the divine union. For precious seconds, only Elowen existed, pure, powerful, and united with her mortal lover in defiance of cosmic law.

When awareness returned, Caelin convulsed on the stairs. Her body arched in a painful transformation. Wings of violet flame had partially manifested from her shoulders, burning through her clothing and scorching the steps beneath her. Her skin had gone translucent, internal organs visible through flesh now more light than matter. From her throat came sounds no human vocal cords could produce, harmonies that spoke of stars being born and dying in the same breath.

She was becoming Elowen entirely, her mortal self burning away like mist in the desert sun.

With the last remnants of her human will, she reached for the Ashwell water. Her fingers, now more energy than flesh, passed through the vial at the first attempt. She concentrated, forcing herself to remember the sensation of solid form, of boundaries and limitations.

"Caelin," she croaked between celestial harmonies. "I am Caelin."

Her fingers solidified just enough to grasp the vial. She brought it to lips that flickered between human and divine and drank deeply, too deeply. Half the remaining water was gone in a desperate attempt to hold on to her humanity.

The effect was immediate and violent. The partially manifested wings retracted with a sound like thunder, divine fire retreating into human flesh that couldn't possibly contain it. She screamed as mortality reasserted itself, the pain of forced compression driving her to the edge of consciousness. The Underspire rippled around her, responding to her agony with tremors that shook the very foundations of the space.

When the transformation subsided, she lay trembling on the stairs, tears streaming from eyes that had glimpsed the universe in its totality. Only a quarter of the Ashwell water remained. One more sip, perhaps two, if she was extremely careful.

It wouldn't be enough. Not for what waited at the heart of the Underspire.

With renewed urgency, Caelin forced herself to her feet. The soulmark beneath her collarbone pulsed with desperate intensity, reminding her of what was at stake. Above her, Lucan's presence had dimmed to barely a whisper.

***

The last chamber opened before her like a flower blooming in the space of a single heartbeat. She stepped through its threshold into paradise itself.

She had to reach the silver-rooted tree before it was too late, before she lost either her humanity to divine transformation or Lucan to the void that claimed forgotten souls.

It pulsed with living light, each leaf catching and reflecting moments from Elowen's existence like faceted gems holding captured stars. The trunk stretched impossibly high, lost in the cavern's glowing ceiling, while roots extended deep into reality's foundation itself. She could see memories moving through its branches like sap made of crystallized time, every preserved mortal moment, every divine choice, every heartbreak and triumph that had shaped existence across countless ages.

Electric tension charged the air, each breath a heady mix of potential and fate. It tingled on her tongue, sending shivers across her skin and awakening something ancient within her. Her divine essence thrummed in resonance, both exhilarated and daunted by the familiarity of this place. Around her, silver bark shimmered like moonlight captured in wood, while leaves glowed softly, casting ethereal patterns that whispered of forgotten realms and celestial duties fulfilled.

The soulmark beneath her collarbone blazed with such intensity that light spilled through her clothing, casting violet shadows across the cavern floor. Lucan's presence was now barely perceptible, a fading echo that threatened to dissolve completely if she didn't act soon.

Three paths shimmered before the tree, each one calling to different aspects of her fractured identity. She understood with absolute clarity that touching those silver roots would force her to choose not just between remembering and forgetting but between three fundamental versions of herself:

The careful mortal Caelin who'd built a life among fragments, never quite understanding why she felt incomplete.

The divine Elowen who'd shattered heaven for love, whose power could reshape reality itself but at terrible cost.

Or something entirely new, a being who honestly integrated both natures without losing either, who could balance memory and choice, divinity and humanity, in ways neither Caelin nor Elowen could alone.

The tree pulsed, waiting. Above, far above, Lucan's connection grew so thin she could barely perceive it at all.

Her choice would determine not just her own fate but his, and possibly the cosmic balance Nerien had sacrificed everything to maintain. Would she choose the safety of mortal limitation, the overwhelming power of divine nature, or the uncharted territory of genuine integration?

The first path glowed with soft amber light, promising the comfort of continued mortal existence. She could return to Caelin's life, with its scholarly pursuits and manageable scope. But the memories would fade again, and with them, the bond that kept Lucan anchored to existence.

The second path blazed with violet fire, offering full restoration of Elowen's divine power. She could reclaim her place in the cosmic order, challenge Nerien on equal terms, and reshape reality according to her will. But such power might burn away everything human within her, including the capacity for the very love that had driven her to rebellion.

The third path shimmered with an iridescent light that contained both violet and amber, neither dominant nor submissive. This was the hardest path, requiring her to carry contradictions, to embrace both divine responsibility and human vulnerability, to find strength in limitation and humility in power.

The Underspire trembled around her, waiting for a choice that would reshape everything.

Caelin reached toward the silver roots, her decision crystallizing as her fingers brushed against bark that felt like memory itself made tangible.

# CHAPTER 11
# THE TRUTH OF MEMORY

The silver tree beckoned her, its voice resonating like the purest notes of starlight crystallized into sound.

As Caelin approached the tree, her vision blurred, reality splitting into overlapping images. One moment she saw through human eyes, the next through divine perception that registered spectrums beyond mortal comprehension. The shift between perspectives sent daggers of pain through her skull, each transition more violent than the last.

She stumbled, falling to her knees halfway across the cavern. The ground pulsed beneath her, responding to her distress with ripples of sympathetic energy. Her hands pressed against her temples where pressure built like steam in a sealed vessel, threatening to shatter her skull from within.

"Hold on," she gasped, fishing out the vial of Ashwell water with trembling fingers. Only a quarter remained, precious drops of reality's anchor. She allowed herself the smallest sip, just enough to force the fractured perspectives back into alignment.

The water burned going down, her increasingly divine system rejecting its mortal properties. For several heartbeats it seemed to have no effect, her vision continuing to oscillate wildly between human and celestial sight. Then, gradually, the perspectives merged into something she could process, not purely mortal and not fully divine but a hybrid perception that allowed her to function.

With each step Caelin took across the cavern floor, the ground beneath her pulsed with a vibrant glow. Liquid light rippled outward from her footfalls, illuminating the space with soft radiance.

Above her, far above, Lucan's presence flickered like a candle struggling against an unseen breeze. Their bond stretched dangerously thin, a single thread where once there had been a rope. Each beat of her heart drew him closer to fading entirely from existence. She had little time.

The silver tree loomed before her, its bark gleaming with metallic brilliance. Intricate glyphs danced across its surface, ancient divine script rearranging itself with each passing moment. These weren't the fragmentary symbols she'd spent years painstakingly cataloging. These were living words that contained complete cosmic truths. The roots spiraled downward, merging seamlessly with the stone beneath, anchoring not just the tree but reality itself.

***

Without hesitation, Caelin pressed both palms flat against the silver bark.

The world shattered.

Not into pieces but into versions, multiple Caelins, multiple Elowens, all screaming for dominance in a single consciousness too fragile to contain them. Divine memories crashed through her mind like tidal waves against a paper boat, threatening to dissolve the very self that experienced them.

"I am..." she tried to speak, but whose voice was it? The scholar's careful diction fractured as celestial harmonics overwhelmed her vocal cords, blood trickling from her nose as capillaries burst under the pressure of containing divinity.

She felt herself unraveling, mortal consciousness dissolving under the onslaught of divine memory. The soulmark beneath her collarbone burned with such intensity that her skin became translucent, organs briefly visible through flesh suddenly more light than matter. Wings of violet flame threatened to erupt from her shoulders, reality warping around the potential manifestation.

With desperate strength, she tore herself away from the tree, falling backward onto the cavern floor. The sudden disconnection left her gasping, blood streaming from her eyes and ears as her system struggled to process what it had contacted.

The vial of Ashwell water trembled in her hand and only a few precious drops remained. Barely enough for one last defense against complete dissolution. She hesitated, knowing that once it was gone, nothing would stand between her and total transformation.

Above her, Lucan's presence flickered dangerously, nearly extinguished.

"I have to continue," she whispered, her voice oscillating between human speech and divine resonance. She uncorked the vial and held the last drops on her tongue, not swallowing immediately but letting the water's essence infuse her awareness.

As the last drops of Ashwell water slid down her throat, she felt a moment of perfect clarity, not suppression of her divine nature but true integration. The water didn't extinguish Elowen's memories but created a structure through which Caelin could experience them without being consumed.

With newfound determination, she pressed her hands against the silver bark once more.

Memory crashed into her consciousness like a dam bursting, not gentle visions or careful fragments but complete immersion in moments too vast for mortal minds to contain.

She stood atop the Sanctum Pinnacle as Elowen, wings of violet flame spread against a star-drunk sky, their span vast enough to embrace mountains. Lucan's hand clasped in hers burned with mortal warmth against her celestial fire as they spoke words that would remake reality itself.

"I vow by light and memory unbound," her own voice rang out, each word carrying the weight of cosmic rebellion, "to choose love over law, devotion over duty. Let heaven itself break before this bond does and let the earth remember what the sky forgets."

"I vow by flesh and will and mortal breath," Lucan replied, his voice steady despite the madness of what they dared, "to stand beside divinity not as subject but as equal, to love without fear what I have sworn to guard. Let death itself unravel before I forsake this choice."

The moment their vows sealed, divine fire erupted between them with such violence that Caelin's mortal consciousness reeled. Not the gentle glow of controlled celestial power but something wild and unprecedented, a conflagration that spoke of laws rewritten and boundaries destroyed. Their soulmarks ignited into existence with such force that reality screamed its protest, the very air splitting like fabric torn by desperate hands.

Above them, the sky cracked like an eggshell, struck by a tremendous blow. Stars fell like burning tears while others blazed brighter than ever before, freed from the careful harmonies that had governed their existence since creation's first breath. The cosmic order that held the heavens in perfect balance simply...ceased.

She saw the Chorus shatter inside her own divine essence, harmony fracturing along the lines of their joined defiance. The divine song that held reality in careful balance broke apart with a sound like every bell ever forged ringing at once before falling silent forever.

*"Elowen."*

Nerien's voice cut through the chaos like a blade of sorrow. They stood before her, silver light streaming from wings that cast no shadow, robes of dusk and starlight billowing in winds that belonged to no earthly realm. Through Elowen's divine sight, Caelin saw clearly the anguish carved across features too perfect for human understanding.

This wasn't divine wrath come to punish transgression. This was a heart breaking under the weight of necessary judgment.

"Sister." The word carried millennia of shared purpose. Twin-forged harmony shattered in a single moment of what Nerien could see only as betrayal. Tears of liquid silver streamed down their luminous face. "You would fracture our balance for mortal flesh? Break the very foundation of what we are? Do you understand what your choice will release into the realms?"

Caelin experienced Elowen's response, divine defiance blazing through celestial awareness like wildfire. "I choose to grow rather than remain perfect. I choose love that changes me over duty that leaves me empty."

"I will carry law alone from the moment you spoke that vow," Nerien cried, their voice breaking. "Judgment without memory to temper it, order without choice to guide it. Do you understand what you will ask me to become? What your love will force me to bear?"

But Elowen had been beyond hearing pleas, intoxicated by forbidden choice and love that refused every boundary.

"Then fall," Nerien announced, the words torn from their throat like pieces of their own heart, "and see what your choosing costs us all!"

Silver fire erupted from Nerien's hands, not aimed at destruction but at separation, at preserving cosmic order through any means necessary. Divine light meant to sever the impossible connection between celestial and mortal, to restore the balance that held reality stable.

But Lucan threw himself between them.

The memory hit Caelin with such devastating force that she collapsed against the tree, her mortal body convulsing. Through Elowen's awareness, she experienced every sensation as Nerien's silver fire struck mortal flesh like a forge hammer against glass.

His ribs cracked. His spine snapped. Blood filled her mouth as their bond transmitted every moment of his breaking. His essence began slipping away, the golden light of his portion of their soulmark flickering with each faltering heartbeat.

But it was his eyes that destroyed her. Dark gaze finding hers even as mortality fled his shattered frame, consciousness fading yet still fixed on her face with desperate tenderness. Blood spilled from a mouth that had spoken vows no mortal should dare, staining lips that tried to smile even as death claimed him.

"Worth it," he gasped, each word a struggle. "All of it, Elowen. For you. For this. Would choose...again..."

His eyes never left her face as the light faded from them. Even dying, broken beyond any hope of healing, he held her gaze with devotion so complete it transcended death by choosing it willingly rather than abandoning what mattered most.

Then his heart stopped. No last word. No grand gesture. Just the most courageous man she'd ever known, choosing her over his own existence and finding peace in that choice, even as it killed him.

***

The grief was complete enough to unmake reality itself. Caelin screamed as she lived through Elowen's reaction, divine fire pouring from her like tears made of liquid starlight. Her wings crumbled to ash around them, each feather dissolving as divinity bled from her transformed flesh.

"No," she keened, the sound shattering windows in the city far below. "No, come back. You don't get to die for me. You don't get to leave me here with this choice, alone with the weight of what we've done." Her hands pressed against his chest where no heartbeat answered her desperate touch. "Come back, Lucan. Please. I'll take it all back. I'll forget you. I will be what they want. Just come back."

But the dead do not return for bargaining, no matter how divine the voice that pleads with them.

Above them both, Nerien wept silver tears that fell like rain across the ruined Pinnacle.

"I cannot undo what is done," they said, voice breaking under the weight of cosmic consequence and personal loss. Through Elowen's divine perception, Caelin felt Nerien's agony as clearly as her own, a twin-forced sibling watching their other half break for a love neither had understood until it destroyed everything they'd built together.

Yet in that moment of mutual agony, something shifted in Nerien's divine countenance. Where there had been only law's rigid certainty, compassion bloomed. Not weakness but a deeper strength born from witnessing suffering they would have once dismissed as merely the consequence of transgression.

"But I can spare you the pain of remembering."

The erasure that followed wasn't the cruel imprisonment Caelin had expected. It was the deepest mercy Nerien could offer, divine love finding its purest expression in the willingness to bear an impossible burden alone rather than watch their sister suffer beneath its weight.

Silver fire washed over her consciousness, not burning but dissolving, separating memory from identity until only an empty vessel remained. Nerien worked with infinite precision, preserving Elowen's essential nature while removing every trace of the choice that had shattered them both.

"Forget," Nerien said through tears that never stopped falling, their own anguish bleeding through the working. "Forget the choice that broke heaven. Forget the love that cost everything. Forget what you were, who you were, why you fell. Sleep in blessed ignorance while I carry our burden alone."

"Live small," they continued, voice thick with the promise of protection bought through sacrifice. "Live safe. Live mortal and content and never know what we paid for your moment of beautiful, terrible love."

The last thing Elowen saw before the erasure completed was Nerien cradling her fading form with infinite gentleness, twin-forged sibling choosing duty over desire, law over love, cosmic stability over everything that made existence worth pre-serving. They were magnificent in their grief, terrible in their mercy, broken beyond any hope of healing, but still functioning because someone had to keep the realms from falling into chaos.

"When you wake," Nerien promised, pressing a kiss to her forehead that burned like benediction and farewell combined, "you will be Caelin Wenriel, and the name Elowen will be just another glyph in ancient texts. You will live and age and die as mortals do, without ever knowing what your choice unmade."

Then darkness. Then forgetting. Then waking in a world that no longer remembered what she'd been.

***

The memory released Caelin with the force of a physical blow. She collapsed against the silver tree, sobbing as the full weight of divine recollection threatened to shatter her mortal consciousness. She understood now the true scope of what had been lost, what Nerien had sacrificed, and what love had cost them all.

Without the Ashwell water's protection, the transformation accelerated. Her skin glowed from within, blood turning to liquid light in her veins. The cavern warped around her, reality struggling to accommodate a being shifting between states of existence. Her perception expanded beyond the physical, sensing cosmic forces that flowed through the very foundation of the Underspire.

"No," she gasped, fighting against the dissolution of her human self. "Not yet. Not before I choose."

***

With monumental effort, she forced her consciousness to remain integrated, not Caelin drowning beneath Elowen's power, not Elowen burning away Caelin's humanity, but both identities held in precarious balance. The effort left her trembling, curled against the silver tree as waves of transformation washed through her.

Her soulmark blazed beneath her collarbone, violet light streaming through her clothing to illuminate the cavern floor. The bond with Lucan stretched so thin she could barely perceive it now, a whisper where once had been a shout, a single thread about to snap. He was dying again, fading back into whatever void claimed the forgotten dead, sustained only by her memory and choice.

***

Three paths unfurled from the tree's roots, each radiating a different allure.

The first path glimmered with amber warmth, beckoning like an old friend. This was the path of humanity, where Caelin Wenriel could shed her celestial mantle entirely, divine powers and ethereal memories slipping away like whispers in a breeze. Lucan would dissolve into whatever lay beyond death's veil, leaving her to embrace uncomplicated mortal life, unburdened by cosmic duties. It would honor Nerien's sacrifice, accepting their gift as the mercy it was intended to be.

The second path blazed with violet brilliance so intense it seared the eyes. This was the path of divinity, where Elowen could reclaim her full godhood, shedding the lessons gained through her mortal journey. She could ascend to the Chorus alone, embracing both memory and law as Nerien had done, yet at the cost of relinquishing every human insight that had kindled her capacity for love. Raw power untempered by the richness of human experience.

The third path shimmered with subtle iridescence, a delicate filament of light that almost escaped notice. This was the path of integration, a daring fusion where Elowen's ethereal essence would merge with Caelin's earthly resilience. This path promised something unprecedented, celebrating both celestial and human aspects without losing either. Yet it demanded immense fortitude to balance divine brilliance with mortal gravity, ensuring neither overwhelmed the other.

As she contemplated her choice, the silver tree began shedding leaves, each one a luminescent tear cascading to the earth. They shimmered briefly before vanishing, Lucan's memories slipped away as their tether frayed into nothingness. The tree's branches withered, curling inward as if suffocated by dwindling possibilities. Time was running out.

"I refuse to choose between my past self and who I am now," Caelin declared to the wilting tree, her voice resonating with a celestial command that belied her tears. "They are not rival souls vying for control but facets of one spirit striving to blend in harmony."

As she spoke, her form fluctuated violently, one moment solid and human, the next luminous and divine. Without the

Ashwell water to stabilize her, the transformation threatened to overwhelm her completely. Her features blurred, shifting between Caelin's scholarly countenance and Elowen's celestial perfection.

Divine awareness flooded through her mind with such force that she cried out, dropping to her knees as cosmic knowledge threatened to overwrite human understanding. The memories came faster now, watching civilizations rise and fall, stars being born and dying, the intricate patterns of reality itself unfolding before divine perception.

"Both," she gasped through the pain of transformation. "I need to be both."

Her body radiated light so intensely that the cavern walls reflected it back like mirrors, creating an endless recursion of illumination. The silver tree responded, its branches extending toward her as though reaching for a long-lost child. Where the tips touched her skin, divine fire and mortal flesh negotiated a new reality, neither fully celestial nor entirely human.

"I am Caelin Wenriel, who learned to catalog beauty among fragments and build meaning from broken things. Who understands the value of small kindnesses and patient restoration." Her voice strengthened with each word, though it echoed with harmonics no human throat could produce. "I am also Elowen, who chose love over law and growth over stagnation, who learned that some things matter more than cosmic order."

The transformation reached its crescendo, her mortal body unable to contain the divine power surging through it, her divine essence unwilling to relinquish the humanity it had learned to value. For one terrifying moment, she existed in the perfect balance between dissolution and integration, poised at the edge of either destruction or transcendence.

Then something shifted within the very fabric of her being. Not rejection of either nature but true synthesis. The violet flame of her divine self wrapped around her human core like protective wings, while her mortal consciousness provided grounding and perspective to celestial power. Neither nature dominant nor submissive, both essential to what she was becoming.

She embodied the essence of memory and law, seamlessly intertwined yet guided by her own decisions. Love tempered her power, though immense, a divine force brought to life through a mortal's grasp of beauty and the inevitable pain of loss. Each deliberate step in Caelin's meticulous journey lent depth to Elowen's celestial presence, while every flicker of heavenly insight deepened her human empathy.

The silver tree shimmered with sudden brilliance, its once-fading leaves unfurling into lush splendor. The Underspire pulsed with awareness, its ancient essence resonating with her newfound presence. No longer was she a remnant of divinity grasping for past grandeur; instead, she embodied a harmonious blend of celestial grace and earthly compassion, weaving together the threads of law and love without compromise.

The world shifted around her, not with chaos but with fulfillment. The test had reached its end. Truth had chosen its bearer.

The cavern walls contracted rhythmically, like a newly awakened heart. She needed to return to Lucan quickly, before the fragile thread of their bond snapped irreparably. And she had to confront Nerien as something unexpected, a testament that love and law could intertwine when decisions were guided by wisdom rather than defiance.

The Underspire released her with a sound like singing crystal, and she began her ascent toward whatever waited above.

# CHAPTER 12

# THE CONFRONTATION

The temperature plummeted like a stone dropped into an abyss.

Lucan stumbled backward from the sealed Deeping Gate as frost erupted across the ancient stones in crystalline spirals, each pattern precise as divine mathematics made manifest. The cold bit through his already tenuous form like daggers of winter air, and his breath emerged as silver mist that hung motionless in an atmosphere suddenly thick with otherworldly presence.

"Something vast approaches," the Watcher said, their voice carrying harmonics that resonated through the cavern walls like the tolling of bells cast from melted stars. For the first time since Lucan had encountered this mysterious guardian, uncertainty crept into their tone, ancient and bone-deep. "Powers that dwarf mortal comprehension draw near."

Jalen pressed himself against the far wall, his scholarly satchel clutched to his chest with white-knuckled desperation. Sweat beaded on his forehead despite the plummeting temperature.

"The resonance signatures," he stammered, terror transforming his voice into barely recognizable whispers. "Multiple entities moving through the upper tunnels with coordinated purpose. Divine-class manifestations. I can feel them pressing against reality itself."

"What resonance signatures?" Lucan demanded, though his marked eye blazed with golden warning light, the divine ring flaring as it recognized the approaching power that matched its own celestial origins.

Before Jalen could form an answer, reality shattered.

Silver radiance poured through the chamber's entrance like liquid starlight given weight and substance, carrying harmonics that bypassed mortal hearing to resonate directly in the marrow of bones. The ancient stones cried out in voices not heard since their first shaping as cosmic force pressed against mortal architecture never designed to contain such magnitude of power. Protective wards carved deep into the walls flared white-hot before fracturing with sounds like screaming crystal.

Nerien manifested in the chamber like winter's heart given form.

They moved without the crude necessity of walking, their resplendent presence too intense for human perception to process without pain. Reality bent around them like light seeking an alternative path, while robes woven from ash and captured starlight billowed in winds that carried the scent of distant nebulae. Where their form touched stone, frost spread in geometric patterns that spoke of mathematical perfection rather than natural cold, each ice crystal a miniature embodiment of cosmic law made visible.

The very air shimmered with barely contained authority, the accumulated weight of divine responsibility carried alone for millennia until it brooked no opposition, no compromise, and no deviation from the order that held existence stable.

"Step away from the threshold, revenant," Nerien commanded, their voice cutting through the chamber like crystal bells tuned to frequencies that made mortal minds reel with existential dread. Each word carried the weight of cosmic mandate, reality reshaping itself slightly to accommodate divine will made audible. "Your trespass against natural order ends now."

Behind them, beings of geometric light and crystalline law emerged from the entrance tunnel like living mathematics given purpose and form. They moved in perfect coordination, each entity humming with power that made the surrounding stone tremble in harmonic resonance. These were not the crude matter and energy of mortal realms, but embodiments of principle itself, cosmic constants taking shape to serve divine will.

Lucan's form flickered under the assault of concentrated celestial presence. Without Caelin's constant choice to anchor his existence, proximity to beings of true divine nature proved catastrophic for his tenuous hold on coherence. Color bled from his features like watercolor in rain as his revenant nature struggled against an environment that rejected his possibility.

"I won't abandon her," he managed through teeth that clicked together. "Not again. Never again."

"You possess no authority in this matter." Nerien raised one alabaster hand, silver fire gathering around their fingers like captured pieces of dying stars, each spark containing enough energy to rewrite local causality. "Defiance of natural law forged what binds you to mortal realms."

"I speak dissolution, and you will return to whatever void claims those who overstay death's invitation."

The silver fire lanced toward Lucan's chest where the soul-mark blazed with increasingly desperate light. Divine energy meant to unmake, to reduce complex existence to component elements that could be sorted back into proper categories. But before the celestial assault could complete its killing work, ash gray robes billowed between them as the Watcher stepped forward with fluid grace.

The silver fire struck the Watcher's extended palm and simply ceased. Not deflected or absorbed, but consumed utterly, leaving no trace save a faint shimmer that ran along the guardian's concealed features like captured moonlight.

"You will not unmake him while I maintain vigil," the Watcher said, their voice carrying depths that suggested caverns vast enough to echo with the sorrows of ages. "Not while any fragment of devotion remains to shield what love has preserved."

***

Nerien's too-bright form went absolutely motionless, divine attention focusing with the intensity of a star's gravity. "You dare interfere with cosmic judgment? You, who exist only as echo and self-inflicted torment?"

"I exist because mortal flesh proved insufficient when divinity required salvation." The Watcher turned slightly, their concealed features somehow conveying both accusation and profound understanding as they regarded Lucan with recognition older than memory. "I am what remained when your divine fire broke his body and scattered his essence across the realms. The fragment that could not forgive its failure when love demanded the impossible."

Understanding struck Lucan with the force of the revelation. His partially translucent features, twisted in horror and recognition combined as pieces of himself he hadn't known were missing, suddenly clicked into place. The emptiness he'd carried since awakening, not just missing memories but missing self.

"You're part of me," he whispered, voice breaking. "The part that stayed behind, watching, remembering what I couldn't save."

"The part that witnessed her burning wings dissolve to ash while you lay broken on scorched stone, helpless to shield her from consequence." The Watcher's voice carried the accumulated weight of centuries spent in self-imposed penance, each word polished smooth by endless repetition in the silence of a solitary vigil. "I have stood at this threshold since the moment you failed her, bearing responsibility for that instant so you could exist without being crushed beneath its memory."

Lucan staggered as if physically struck. His hand reached toward the Watcher, toward himself, fingers trembling as they passed through the guardian's insubstantial form. The weight of centuries of separation, of fractured existence, of incomplete understanding slammed into him with devastating clarity.

"All this time," he breathed, "I wasn't whole. Not just missing memories but missing part of my very soul."

***

"A soul fragment cannot persist independently," Jalen interrupted, his scholarly instincts momentarily overcoming terror. "This violates every principle of spiritual mechanics. Divine magic doesn't permit such configurations."

"Divine magic bends to accommodate whatever love proves strong enough to demand," Nerien replied, their attention fixed on the Watcher with something approaching painful recognition. "When mortal will refuses every ending death offers, it discovers methods of endurance that transcend our most fundamental understanding of how existence functions."

They gestured to the crystalline beings arrayed around the chamber's perimeter like living pillars of cosmic order. "We cannot permit such defiance to spread unchecked. Stability must be maintained. The barriers between realms must hold against chaos that would consume everything we have built."

One of the geometric entities stepped forward, its form cycling through mathematical configurations that caused physical pain to observe directly. When it spoke, its voice carried absolute precision, stripped of every trace of emotion or personal investment.

"Jalen Mor of the Order of Preservation. You were tasked with monitoring and documenting anomalous divine manifestations under established protocols. Instead, you have aided the very forces you swore to contain and redirect toward authorized channels."

Jalen's face drained of blood until his skin appeared as translucent as parchment. His fingers tightened around his satchel as months of internal conflict played across his features, the scholar's curiosity warring with institutional loyalty, the preservationist's commitment to safety battling against the human capacity for empathy.

"I swore nothing to entities like you," he finally said, straightening his shoulders despite the tremor in his voice. "I believed I was working for mortal preservation societies, scholars dedicated to protecting heritage and knowledge, not for this." He gestured weakly at the assembled celestial forces that made the surrounding air shimmer with barely contained power. "Not whatever this represents."

"The Order of Preservation was established under my authority centuries past," Nerien said, their tone carrying the accumulated weight of cosmic disappointment. "Created to monitor mortal realms for any sign that the Collapsed divine essence might attempt restoration. You have served faithfully for years, documenting every anomaly, every sign that she stirred toward wakefulness."

***

"So you could erase her again," Lucan snarled, his form solidifying with a fury that temporarily overcame the divine pressure threatening to tear his existence apart. His soulmark blazed gold through his tattered shirt, pulsing in defiance of the void that beckoned. "So you could unmake what we rebuilt from the ashes of your judgment."

"So I could spare her the devastating agony of remembering what her choice unleashed," Nerien replied, silver flames beginning to gather around their entire form like a corona of sorrow and infinite loss. Their voice fractured with the weight of millennia spent in solitary duty. "Do you comprehend what I have carried alone since the moment you spoke those catastrophic vows? Law without memory to temper harsh judgment. Order without choice to provide direction. The crushing burden of maintaining cosmic stability while my other half pursued desires that broke the very foundations we were created to protect."

The chamber trembled as Nerien's power built toward manifestation that would reshape local reality according to their will. Hairline cracks appeared in ancient stone walls, spreading like blood vessels as mortal architecture proved inadequate to contain the full presence of cosmic authority made manifest.

"She chose love over law, growth over eternal stagnation," they continued, their voice breaking with grief accumulated across centuries of absolute solitude. "And I was forced to become law without love's guidance, order without growth's possibilities, everything she abandoned in her moment of magnificent, devastating selfishness."

"She chose to become something greater than either of you had been separately," the Watcher said with a quiet conviction that carried more weight than a shouted argument. "As did he. What you interpret as cosmic defiance, they understood as necessary evolution."

"Evolution that shattered the fundamental framework holding existence in stable configuration!" Silver fire erupted outward from Nerien's form with enough violence to pulverize stone, striking the chamber walls and leaving molten scars glowing with residual divine energy. "Observe what surrounds us. The Underspire itself, constructed from fragments of reality their love destroyed. Existence remade around the crater their choice carved in the heart of ordered cosmos."

***

Lucan staggered as the divine assault intensified, his form flickering like a candle buffeted by hurricane winds that carried the scent of burning stars. The connection stretching down to Caelin far below grew gossamer-thin with each moment of exposure, strained beyond its design limits by proximity to power that denied his right to exist.

He pressed one increasingly translucent hand to his chest where the soulmark blazed with the desperate light of a signal fire in hostile darkness. The golden glow pulsed erratically now, weakening with each beat. Without Caelin's conscious choice to anchor him, he was unraveling back into scattered components.

"Caelin," he whispered, focusing all his remaining strength on their connection. "Whatever trial you face in the depths, please find your answers quickly. I cannot maintain this coherence much longer."

As if responding to his fervent call, a fresh glow emerged beyond the closed Deeping Gate. It wasn't the sharp silver that marked Nerien's dominion or the comforting gold of human faith. Instead, this light blended violet with both hues, creating an illumination that whispered of unity rather than separation. It was a choice made with full awareness, not one born from fiery rebellion and blind ignorance.

The Gate's ancient substance began resonating with power, causing even Nerien to retreat a measured step, divine recognition warring with growing alarm across features too bright for human perception.

"Impossible," they breathed, silver fire faltering around their luminous form like dying stars. "The erasure was absolute. She was meant to remain mortal, shielded from the burden of godly accountability, living and dying without divine interference."

The resonance beyond the Gate built toward a crescendo that made the entire chamber vibrate like a bell struck by cosmic forces, stones singing in harmonies that predated language. Reality itself held its breath in that moment of perfect tension, when existence balanced on the edge of transformation that could either heal ancient wounds or tear them wider than ever before.

***

And in that crystalline instant of suspended possibility, the Deeping Gate dissolved like morning mist before sunrise.

Light poured through the widening aperture, not the harsh brilliance of unleashed power seeking to overwhelm and dominate but something infinitely deeper, warmer, carrying the promise of dawn after the longest night in memory. Walking through that radiance with steps that made reality sing in recognition came Caelin Wenriel.

She moved with the precise grace of the scholar merged with the ethereal presence of divinity, neither aspect dominating, neither diminished. Her eyes held the accumulated wisdom of centuries past and the immediate compassion of a woman who understood mortality's precious brevity. Where her feet touched stone, tiny violets bloomed impossibly from solid rock, each petal vibrant with a life that defied natural law without breaking it.

Her soulmark blazed beneath her collarbone, violet light streaming through her clothing to illuminate the chamber with radiance that carried neither judgment nor defiance but something entirely new. Integration made visible, balance made flesh.

Nerien's silver fire dimmed in recognition of something they had never imagined possible. Not Elowen returned to challenge their rule, not Caelin elevated to godhood but a genuine third path that refused the binary choice between divine and mortal nature.

"Sibling," Caelin said, her voice layered with harmonic depths that made the chamber's stones vibrate in sympathetic resonance. "I have remembered. But I have not forgotten."

# Chapter 13

# The Integration

Reality bowed in recognition.

Caelin stepped through the dissolved Deeping Gate, and the chamber sang. Ancient stones hummed with harmonies that predated language, while glyphs carved into the walls flared with sudden purpose. Each footfall sent ripples of controlled power racing across the floor, not the wild defiance that had once shattered heaven but authority earned through the willing synthesis of opposing natures.

She moved with a fluidity that spoke of profound transformation. Gone was the careful precision of the mortal restorer, replaced by grace that made the surrounding space adjust to accommodate her passage. Gone too was the terrible perfection of Elowen's celestial beauty. What remained was something unprecedented: divine power tempered by human wisdom, cosmic authority rooted in the understanding that some things mattered more than eternal order.

Violets bloomed where she stepped, petals unfurling from solid stone before cycling into fertile ash that glowed with residual starlight. The transformation spoke of integration rather than dominance and growth guided by choice rather than imposed by will.

***

"Caelin." Lucan's voice cracked with desperate relief as her presence touched their bond. Color flooded back through his translucent form like sunrise driving away the longest night. His fractured edges solidified, pale skin warming with the return of substantial flesh as their connection stabilized for the first time since his resurrection.

"I remember everything," she said, crossing to him with steps that made reality sing. "What we were. What we chose. What our love created, and what it cost." Her hands framed his face with infinite tenderness, thumbs tracing the sharp angles where the recent dissolution had threatened to steal him forever. "I know who I am now."

Their bond allowed him to feel the vast integration she had achieved. Not Elowen reborn or Caelin ascending but something unprecedented: two halves of identity fused without the loss of either. Mortal wisdom strengthening divine power, celestial nature grounded in a human understanding of what made existence precious enough to protect.

Across the chamber, Nerien recoiled as though physical proximity to successful synthesis caused them pain.

"The erasure was absolute," they breathed, silver light streaming from their form in ribbons of barely controlled anguish. "Mortal consciousness cannot contain complete divine memory without fragmenting beyond recovery."

"Because you tried to force separation rather than allowing unity," Caelin replied, turning to face her twin-forged sibling with eyes that held depths, both celestial and human. As she spoke, the very stones echoed her words, the ancient architecture recognizing an authority surpassing any it had previously served.

"You understand nothing." Nerien's form blazed brighter, silver fire gathering around their hands like captured pieces of dying stars. "Divine law exists to preserve cosmic order. Memory serves to maintain eternal continuity. These principles cannot be compromised for mortal sentiment."

"Then watch," Caelin said simply.

***

The world crystallized around them like amber preserving a perfect moment. Reality froze midbreath: Nerien's silver assault suspended between intention and impact, cosmic forces locked in temporal stillness, even dust motes hanging motionless in air that had forgotten how to move. Only Caelin and Lucan remained free to act within the bubble of suspended time she'd created through sheer will made manifest.

"Now," she confided, her attention fixing on him with an intensity that made his heart race with renewed velocity. "Before anything else tries to separate us."

His breath caught as understanding flowed between them. This wasn't simply a reunion but the conscious completion of a bond that required deliberate choosing to achieve permanent stability. Around them, frozen reality waited while they claimed the privacy necessary for what came next.

"You're certain?" he asked, though his hands already reached for her with the desperate hunger of someone who'd stared dissolution in the face and found salvation at the last moment.

"More certain than I've ever been about anything," she replied, stepping into his embrace with grace that made the surrounding silence hum with anticipation. "Divine enough to love without fear of consequence. Human enough to choose what matters most."

Her lips met his with the taste of heaven and earth combined, celestial fire tempered by mortality into something that nourished rather than consumed. When his hands found her waist, power flowed between them like honey mixed with liquid starlight, each touch confirming their shared existence in ways that transcended mere physical sensation.

"Your heartbeat," she marveled, pressing her palm to his chest, where life pulsed with renewed strength. "I can sense it through our connection. Faint but real."

"Because you anchored me." His voice roughened with emotion as he traced the line of her throat with reverent fingertips. "Every choice you made in the depths below fed strength into my form when dissolution threatened. You held me together across impossible distance through nothing but determined love."

Her skin carried a subtle luminescence that responded to his touch, growing brighter where their flesh connected as though mortal contact awakened the divine fire she'd learned to contain. Each point of contact sent cascades of sensation through their bond, pleasure magnified by the relief of touching someone they'd nearly lost forever.

"Show me what choosing love feels like," she murmured against his throat, where his pulse hammered with accelerating rhythm.

He answered by drawing her closer, her body fitting against his with the perfection of memory made new. When he pressed her back against stone that hummed with accumulated power, she moved with him in a fluid partnership that spoke of souls learning to share the same rhythm while maintaining individual strength.

The slow removal of barriers between them became a meditation on reverence and desire combined. Each revealed inch of skin carried its own story: the soulmark beneath her shoulder that blazed with violet fire, the place over his heart where golden light pulsed in perfect synchronization. When they came together in the privacy of suspended time, the sensation transcended physical joining to become recognition of two halves achieving completion through choice rather than destiny.

"This is how it was meant to be," Caelin breathed as they moved together in rhythms that made their matching marks flare bright enough to cast dancing shadows across the temporal stillness. "Chosen freely, again and again, until choosing becomes as natural as breathing."

Power flowed between them with each shared heartbeat, divine energy grounded by his mortal understanding, while her celestial nature enhanced his humanity. She felt his wonder at her transformation; he experienced her joy at his complete restoration. Two souls learning to exist in perfect harmony without losing the individual qualities that made their union precious.

When climax claimed them both, their synchronized marks erupted with light that made the frozen chamber ring like crystal bells touched by cosmic wind. The bond between them stabilized, sealed beyond any future attempt at severance by authorities that failed to understand what willing love could accomplish when guided by wisdom rather than driven by mere desire.

As their breathing returned to normal cadence, Caelin waved her hand with casual authority, clothing reappearing on their forms before she released her hold on the temporal flow. Reality resumed its natural rhythm with barely a ripple to mark the private eternity they'd shared.

***

"The vigil ends."

The Watcher's voice drew their attention as frozen time melted back into motion. They stood nearby with movements that suggested millennial patience finally reaching its intended completion. For the first time since Lucan had encountered them, the concealing hood fell back to reveal features that mirrored his own, marked by the accumulated weight of centuries spent in self-imposed penance.

"The part of you that failed her can rest now," the Watcher continued, extending one hand that trembled with longing held in careful check. "She not only survived but transcended what we couldn't prevent. You fought not in vain but as a prelude to understanding we lacked the wisdom to achieve ourselves."

Recognition dawned in Lucan's expression, bringing with it gratitude and profound sorrow for the sacrifice his soul's fragmentation had demanded. "You've been carrying the guilt that should have been mine to bear."

"I carried the memory of that moment so you could exist without being crushed beneath its weight," the Watcher replied. Then they smiled, the expression transforming their careworn features with unexpected peace. "But love proved stronger than failure. Growth transcended loss. My watch is over."

Light poured from the Watcher's dissolving form, flowing into Lucan like sunrise filling a valley long shrouded in darkness. The integration was instantaneous and complete. Missing pieces of his soul found their home, completing restoration that their bond had begun but required this conscious choice to finish.

For the first time since his death centuries past, Lucan felt something fundamental shift within his essence. The fragmented pieces of his soul, the part that had clawed back from death, the part that had maintained vigil, finally existed in the same space again. His breathing deepened from deliberate mimicry to something approaching natural rhythm, though the golden ring marking his right eye still blazed with divine judgment.

"Whole," Caelin breathed, studying his transformed face with eyes bright with shared joy. "You're becoming whole again."

The integration was profound but incomplete. He could feel the Watcher's memories settling into his consciousness like sediment finding the bottom of a clear stream. The centuries of patient vigil, the weight of failure carefully borne, the love that had sustained solitary purpose. Yet something still held him suspended between full life and borrowed existence, awaiting a final transformation that their bond promised but had not yet delivered.

***

Across the chamber, Nerien stood motionless among the geometric beings that served cosmic order, their luminous form trembling with what looked like accumulated despair finally finding voice.

"I have maintained the balance alone for so long," they said, voice fracturing under millennial isolation's weight. "Law without memory to guide mercy. Order without growth to prevent stagnation. I am so very tired of carrying such weight in isolation."

Before anyone could respond to this unprecedented admission of vulnerability, reality twisted around Nerien's will like glass bending under cosmic heat. A surge of energy enveloped them, a tingling sensation dancing across skin and filling the air with shimmering resonance. The chamber dissolved as divine power transported them to the place where everything had begun.

They stood atop the Sanctum Pinnacle, beneath the broken dome where the shattered sky opened directly to eternal stars. Here, where vows had once shattered heaven itself, the ultimate confrontation would unfold under the witness of a cosmos that no longer obeyed the rules governing its creation.

***

The wind howled through the broken dome above, carrying echoes of ancient pain and possibility. Caelin's feet touched the scorched stone that remembered her fall, while Lucan stood exactly where he had died defending their love centuries before. The circle was complete, not as repetition, but as an opportunity for genuine healing.

Nerien's silver fire blazed against the night sky, their form radiant with power accumulated across solitary millennia of maintaining cosmic order alone. Yet now Caelin could see what she'd missed before, the exhaustion beneath brilliance, the loneliness beneath righteousness, the yearning for completion that mirrored her own journey toward integration.

"It doesn't have to end as it began," Caelin said, violet light flowing from her like gentle rain rather than consuming fire. Her hand found Lucan's, their fingers intertwining as their soulmarks pulsed in perfect synchronization. "There is another way, one that honors both law and memory, both order and growth."

Nerien trembled, silver tears streaming down luminous features too perfect for mortal comprehension. "I don't know how to be anything but what I've become," they whispered, voice breaking under the weight of confession. "I've been law without love's guidance for so long."

"Then let me show you," Caelin replied, stepping forward with a hand extended, not in defiance but in offering. "Let me return what was taken from us both."

Above them, stars blazed with unprecedented brilliance, cosmic witnesses to when choice might finally heal what blind rebellion had once broken beyond recognition.

# Chapter 14

# The Sibling's Surrender

T he Sanctum Pinnacle rose like a broken crown against stars that no longer recalled their given names.

Caelin stepped out of Nerien's dimensional transport, feeling the gritty swirl of stone dust around her boots. Moonlight filtered through the shattered dome above, casting silver beams across the ancient Pinnacle. The altar stones lay ahead, their surfaces etched with charred patterns where divine flames had once seared reality. She looked up at the fractured sky, a window into the cosmos that now danced around the crater their vows had etched into existence itself.

Time seemed solid here, suspended in the moment between choice and consequence. Wind that tasted of ozone and distant cosmos whispered through the ruins, carrying echoes of words spoken centuries past, and vows that had broken heaven and remade the fundamental laws governing the relationship between mortal and divine.

"This place remembers," Caelin said, her voice resonating with harmonics that set the surrounding stones gently vibrating in response. With each step, she felt energy rippling beneath her feet, awakening the ancient architecture. Glyphs etched into the towering pillars flickered to life, glowing softly as if nodding in recognition of her presence.

Next to her, Lucan inhaled deeply, as if savoring a gift he had almost lost for good. His hand slipped into hers with the ease of familiarity, their fingers weaving together like strands of an old tapestry. As he surveyed the shattered sanctuary, his gaze was sharp and vigilant, the golden ring in his right eye pulsing with the watchfulness that had once sustained his fragmented soul through centuries of vigil.

"Here," Nerien's voice resonated, their silver light flooding the shattered stones and crumbled masonry with a gentle glow. They appeared at the altar's heart, moving with an elegance that defied gravity, robes woven from dusk and starlight swirling around them in ethereal winds. Those winds carried faint murmurs from realms beyond comprehension. "This is where your words broke the Chorus," Nerien continued, their tone carrying the weight of centuries, "and left me to bear the burden of cosmic law alone, shrouded in solitude."

Behind Caelin and Lucan, Jalen stumbled as divine transportation released him onto solid stone. His scholar's satchel clutched to his chest, he looked between the broken dome and the assembled powers with wonder that had transcended terror to become professional fascination.

"The resonance signatures in this area," he whispered, retrieving instruments that buzzed with the nearby divine energy. "There are layered temporal distortions and reality fluctuations here that existed before any recorded phenomena. This is where the very fabric of existence changed." His fingers moved quickly, documenting what no mortal scholar had ever witnessed, the reconciliation of cosmic forces that might reshape reality itself.

Around the Pinnacle's edge, geometric entities took shape, their forms precise and humming with otherworldly resonance. The air vibrated under their presence, shimmering as if touched by an unseen hand. Each being moved in flawless harmony, aligning themselves like pillars of a celestial structure only they could perceive.

Nerien's gaze pierced through the air, a brightness so intense it warped the world around them. Caelin felt the heat of their eyes, drawing her in with the gravity of shared origin. Silver flames swirled around Nerien's hands, each flicker like a fragment of a star on the brink of fading away.

"You remember this place," they continued, pain bleeding through divine composure for the first time since manifestation. "You remember the exact moment when our perfect harmony shattered, when memory chose growth over stability, when love proved more important than the cosmic order we maintained."

"I remember choosing to become something greater than eternal perfection," Caelin replied, her integrated nature allowing her to speak with an authority that made reality itself pay attention. Around her, violet light responded to her presence, not the wild defiance of centuries past but power tempered by wisdom. "I remember learning some things matter more than unchanging law."

"And I remember the silence that followed," Nerien said, their voice fracturing with accumulated grief. Silver flames danced higher around their form, each flicker carrying the weight of millennia spent enforcing divine law without memory's tempering guidance. "When your half of the Chorus simply ceased, leaving only echoes and emptiness where harmony once existed."

A biting chill filled the air as Nerien's power pulsed. Frost crept over the ancient stones, forming intricate patterns that seemed more like celestial blueprints than mere ice. Each crystal appeared to be a tiny fragment of the universe's hidden order, etched into existence under Caelin's watchful gaze.

"Do you comprehend what your choice forced me to become?" Nerien's voice carried the accumulated weight of centuries spent in isolation so complete it had hardened into tyranny. "Law without memory becomes rigid doctrine. Order without growth becomes stagnation. I became everything we swore never to allow, authority untempered by compassion."

Lucan moved nearer to Caelin, his presence a solid shield against the rising tension that seemed to pulse from Nerien's glowing figure. She sensed his guardian instincts activating, every muscle in his body alert and ready. "You opted for solitude," he said, his voice unwavering even as energy crackled around them like a brewing storm. "There were other paths to preserve equilibrium without dismantling everything we created together."

"Other paths?" Nerien's laugh held edges sharp enough to cut reality. "When her love proved strong enough to rewrite the fundamental laws governing existence? When mortal will showed power surpassing divine authority? Observe the solution I offer now."

From Nerien's outstretched hands, a blaze of silver fire surged forth, shattering the ancient altar stones with its sheer force. Caelin watched as the divine energy sliced through the air, not directed at her, but at Lucan. The searing light honed in on him with deadly accuracy, targeting the soulmark etched into his chest, the very mark that tethered him to this mortal world.

"I speak dissolution," Nerien declared, their voice carrying the weight of cosmic mandate that could reshape reality through will alone. "I unmake what was forged in defiance of natural law. Let her love only echoes and dreams, as mortals do."

Caelin watched as the celestial fire struck Lucan with the force of a hammer blow, its silver energy crafted to sever even the most indestructible connections. He staggered backward, gasping for air, his soulmark flaring with a fierce and desperate light. The divine power surged through their bond, corrosive and unyielding, like acid eating away at precious metal.

This time, the unraveling felt final. It wasn't a slow, uncertain fading but a forceful tearing apart that denied him any existence beyond death's reach. His skin turned ashen, drained of all color, as the flames hungrily consumed him, breaking him down into basic elements. His body seemed destined to return to the soil, his stolen moments slipping into nothingness, and his love reduced to an empty gesture that left no mark on the world.

"Lucan!" Caelin's cry held enough anguish to make the broken dome above them ring like struck crystal but more than grief. It carried a fury that had been building since the moment she remembered what Nerien had taken from them both.

Violet flames burst from her shoulders, wings unfurling in a sudden, breathtaking display. It was the first time they had appeared since her fall, and their fierce beauty set the air ablaze around her. Each feather shimmered with an angelic fire that had softened over time but still burned true. The wings stretched wide, their reach so immense they could shield entire cities from heaven's raging storms.

The sight struck Jalen speechless. His scholarly instruments fell forgotten as he witnessed divinity made manifest, wings that belonged to no earthly creature spreading like banners of defiance against cosmic tyranny.

Caelin immediately sensed the toll it took. Her mortal body struggled to harness the divine energy, her willpower the only bridge between them. The celestial force within her yearned to break free, testing the boundaries of a vessel never meant to hold such immense power. Blood trickled down her back where her wings emerged, each droplet sizzling against the stone below.

"You would shield him again," Nerien said, their attack faltering as recognition dawned across features too bright for human perception. "You would manifest your divine nature to protect mortal flesh, exactly as you did when devotion destroyed us both."

"I choose to protect what I love," Caelin replied, wrapping Lucan in wings that blazed while their bond stabilized under her conscious protection. Through the connection, she poured strength directly into his fading form, anchoring him to existence through sheer will. "But this time, I understand the cost."

***

Power gathered around her, a force as intense as the pressure before an earthquake. The very fabric of reality warped and twisted, challenged by the authority she wielded, an authority born from unity rather than defiance. As she spoke once more, her voice rang with harmonics that set the crystalline beings around them vibrating in reluctant recognition.

"You've upheld the law without compassion for far too long, my sibling," she spoke softly, the word *sibling* slipping from her lips with a tenderness not heard since their creation. "Allow me to help bear this weight that has twisted you into something we never intended to be."

"Share?" Nerien's voice shattered into fragments of disbelief. "You speak of sharing what your abandonment forced me to bear alone? Do you comprehend the weight I've carried through eons without you?"

Silver light pulsed around Nerien's form, creating distortions in the air as their composure fractured further.

"Each judgment I rendered alone," Nerien continued, voice rising. "Each civilization I watched crumble beneath necessary law. Each prayer I heard but could not answer with compassion because memory was no longer there to temper my decisions."

Caelin stepped forward, her wings creating ripples in the cosmic energy surrounding them. "I understand more than you know."

"You understand nothing!" Nerien's outburst sent shock waves through the ruined sanctuary. "You chose mortal flesh while I became a monster of pure law. Do you know what it means to extinguish worlds without memory's guidance? To feel billions of lives end beneath your decree and know there was no other choice because balance demanded it?"

The silver being's form wavered, briefly revealing glimpses of countless solitary moments, standing vigil over dying stars, weighing the fates of entire galaxies alone, enforcing cosmic law without the counterbalance that once made their judgments merciful.

"I became the villain in creation's story," Nerien whispered, "precisely because you weren't there to remind me why we created it all."

Caelin's wings trembled but remained extended in invitation. "Then let me remember for us both again."

***

"And risk another abandonment?" Nerien's voice cracked with vulnerability beneath the divine fury. "What happens when your mortal love faces the next impossible choice? Will you tear us apart again?"

Lucan, still sheltered within Caelin's wings, spoke, "The choice was never between love and duty. It was between growth and stagnation."

"Easy words from the cause of our division," Nerien hissed, silver tears continuing to flow.

"Nerien," Caelin said softly, using the name with such tenderness that the geometric beings at the periphery visibly resonated. "I don't offer to return to what we were. I offer something greater, integration that honors what we've both learned in separation. Your order tempered by my memory. My love guided by your law."

"And if I refuse? If I complete what I began and sever your mortal attachment permanently?"

"Then you prove what I've suspected," Caelin replied. "That loneliness has wounded you more deeply than our original separation ever could have."

The silence that followed held the weight of universes being born and dying. Nerien's shoulders slumped slightly, the first sign of yielding in a being who had stood immovable since the cosmos was young.

"There were moments," Nerien admitted, voice barely audible, "when I questioned everything. When judgment felt hollow without you there to witness it. When I looked upon creation and could no longer remember why we breathed it into existence."

Caelin moved closer, their energies beginning to harmonize despite Nerien's resistance.

"I wanted to hate you," Nerien continued. "To believe your choice was purely selfish. But in the silence between stars, I sometimes heard echoes of your laughter and wondered if perhaps you had seen a truth I was too rigid to comprehend."

"Not a truth," Caelin said gently. "A different path, one that could lead us here, to this moment of reconciliation neither of us could have imagined."

Nerien looked from her to Lucan, taking in their completed bond that blazed with stable light.

"If I join with you," Nerien asked, "will I too learn to understand what drove you to choose as you did? Will I feel what makes mortality worth such sacrifice?"

"You'll understand," Caelin promised, "and I'll remember the beauty of cosmic law you've preserved. We'll be neither what we were nor what we've become, but something new, something better."

The offer lingered between them, a fragile promise suspended in the air. Along the edge of the Pinnacle, geometric beings stood motionless, their forms casting intricate shadows on the ground. Above, stars shimmered with anticipation, as if pausing to witness what decision would unfold.

Nerien gazed at the wings, once reduced to ash before their eyes, now restored and vibrant. They marveled at the love that had defied even the harshest divine judgment, a force more potent than any celestial decree. The impossible integration unfolded before them, defying every ancient law they had upheld for countless millennia.

"You broke us," they whispered, perfect composure finally cracking under the pressure of emotions suppressed for centuries. Silver tears streamed down their luminous face like liquid starlight, each drop carrying the accumulated weight of isolation so complete it had become indistinguishable from torment.

"You chose mortal flesh over my heart and made me into everything we swore never to become." Nerien sobbed.

In that moment, a memory surfaced, stark and razor-sharp: Nerien standing alone at the edge of a dying star system, celestial hands outstretched as they methodically severed the bonds between twin planets whose gravities had fallen into destructive resonance. One would survive, one would not. No prayer reached them here at creation's edge, but they felt the billions of consciousnesses extinguishing beneath their decree. They had performed this cosmic surgery countless times since the Chorus fractured, making these terrible judgments without memory's tempering wisdom. "Balance requires sacrifice," they had whispered into the void, their voice breaking on words repeated so often they had become a hollow ritual rather than truth. That night, silver tears had fallen into the cosmic dust for the first time, and Nerien realized even divinity could know loneliness.

***

Caelin moved closer, each step resonating with a familiar hum. "You took on that weight so we could both grasp the truth," she said softly. Her eyes held a gentle intensity that made the surrounding air tremble. "Love and law can be allies when wisdom leads instead of fear. Growth thrives alongside order when choice takes the place of strict rules."

Caelin's hands glowed with a violet-silver light as she reached toward Nerien, the colors swirling together in a dance of unity and peace.

"Let love lead the law, not be shackled by it," she said, her voice rich with wisdom forged in the fires of human trials and celestial insights. "Let our memories illuminate our decisions instead of binding them. Let us find completeness once more, not as we were, but as we are destined to be."

***

The decision crystallized slowly, like ice forming on a calm pond...

Nerien's silver flames flickered briefly before extinguishing completely, revealing the radiant figure underneath. This being had carried the weight of cosmic duty long before mortals walked the earth.

"You would truly share this weight?" they asked, voice barely above a whisper that somehow carried clearly through the mountain air. "You would risk your precious love being tempered by the necessity of divine judgment?"

"I would risk everything," Caelin said simply, "to heal what our original choice divided. To prove that the Chorus can exist in forms we never imagined when we thought perfection meant unchanging."

Nerien looked once more from her to Lucan, taking in the way divine power had learned to serve mortal understanding without losing its essential nature. Something in their too-bright expression shifted, not defeat, but the recognition of a possibility they had never allowed themselves to consider.

Their voice, soft as a breeze at dawn, lingered in the air. "Remember me," they murmured, fading away like mist that vanishes with the first light of day. "Not for standing against your love but for safeguarding all that you had to abandon."

Light cascaded from their diminishing form, a radiant blessing that merged with Caelin's violet flame. Molten silver streamed into the fire, melding with an elegance that crafted a beauty beyond either element alone. As they united, understanding flooded through her, an awareness of the universe's deep mathematical order, the delicate equilibrium sustaining reality, and the profound impact of decisions echoing across endless worlds.

Healing washed over her as Nerien's essence intertwined with hers. Caelin sensed their deep love for the very fabric of existence, a willingness to endure endless solitude to prevent Creation from splintering into chaos. She understood laws were crafted to shield what was precious, and order existed to nurture growth, not stifle it. Even judgment, when guided by the wisdom of memory, could be an act of profound care.

***

The geometric beings shimmered and bowed, their forms melting like frost under the gentle touch of spring's first warm rays. Their mission accomplished, they vanished into the air, leaving a sense of balance in their wake.

As dawn's first light spilled over the Pinnacle, the golden rays filtered through the fractured dome, revealing their incredible achievement. Once, two divine beings clashed in fierce opposition, but now harmony prevailed. Love had forged a bridge between law and memory, allowing cosmic authority to be steered by the understanding that certain things held greater importance than eternal perfection.

Caelin's wings tucked themselves neatly against her back, their vibrant violet feathers slowly turning translucent before vanishing altogether. The transformation had taken its toll; her limbs felt leaden with fatigue, and a thin trail of blood trickled down her spine. Yet, within her eyes shone a newfound wholeness, a sense of unity that shattered all the boundaries they once thought unbreakable.

"It's done," Lucan murmured, awe threading through his words as he gazed at her newly altered appearance. The haunting loneliness that had once clung to Nerien like a shadow had vanished. In its place, Caelin stood with the serene grace of someone who had finally discovered where she belonged in the vast tapestry of the universe.

Jalen approached cautiously, his scholar's curiosity overcoming lingering fear. "The resonance signatures have stabilized," he whispered, checking his instruments with shaking hands. "The patterns suggest a fundamental realignment of cosmic forces, as if reality itself is healing from an ancient wound."

Caelin nodded, feeling the changes rippling outward from the Pinnacle. Integration had created something unprecedented, not a return to what was but the birth of something entirely new. Divine law now flowed through channels tempered by mortal understanding, while human growth found stability in cosmic patterns that had existed since the dawn of time.

"We should return to the city," she said, her voice carrying new depths that made the air vibrate with possibilities. "There's much work to be done."

***

As they stood together on the threshold of a new era, the first ray of sunrise caught the tear tracks on Caelin's face, transforming them into threads of light that seemed to connect the earth below to the broken heaven above, not as division but as a bridge between realms that had always been meant to nurture one another.

# CHAPTER 15

# THE GUARDIAN'S HEART

Dawn painted the shattered dome in shades of gold and rose, but Lucan felt none of its warmth.

Lucan lay on stones still scarred by celestial fire, each breath a fierce testament to life balanced on a knife's edge. Nerien's last assault had tried not just to kill him but to wipe him from memory altogether.

Caelin kneeled beside him, trembling hands tracing the invisible wounds etched into his essence. Through their bond, she felt the places where his identity had been scraped thin, like parchment, nearly erased. His right iris burned with renewed golden fury, divine judgment flaring at the thought that mortal flesh had dared to love.

"Can you heal what they broke?" he asked, though his voice carried the rasp of someone speaking through damaged lungs.

"I can ensure nothing will ever threaten to unmake you again." Her words were both a promise and a warning. What she planned required a level of trust they hadn't reached before.

Lucan felt Caelin's cool palms on his chest, where the soul-mark flickered like a dying flame. As their skin touched, he sensed her power, assessing the damage Nerien had caused with precision. Through their bond, he felt her evaluating not just the visible wounds but the deeper fractures threatening his very being.

"This will hurt," she cautioned, celestial fire forming at her fingertips. "I need to rebuild you from the essence outward, reinforcing every thread of your identity. It will feel like being born and dying at once."

"I trust you," he said, the weight of his words catching her breath. Despite everything—resurrection, doubt, and the threat of fading—his faith in her was unwavering.

Through their bond, he sensed how her integration with Nerien enabled a precise and deliberate restoration. Her consciousness mapped every fracture in his essence before methodically beginning the reconstruction. Her power threaded through him like luminous silk, rewriting the fundamental forces that governed his existence with careful intent.

The healing began at his heart, their bond's deepest anchor. Each pulse sent a strengthening fire through vessels that had survived through sheer will. Golden light wove through his arteries, filling the voids where death had left hollow channels.

Caelin watched in awe as the divine energy meticulously rebuilt every fractured piece of his existence. The light moved with deliberate precision, stitching torn sinews with celestial fire. Where his ribs had cracked under divine assault, golden radiance flowed, fusing bone with a strength surpassing its original form.

But the healing was an agony unlike anything Lucan had endured, even in death. Each thread of celestial fire felt like liquid lightning racing through his veins, burning away the hollow spaces that had sustained his revenant existence and replacing them with something his form struggled to contain. He bit back screams as his bones re-formed with crushing pressure, marrow flooding with the life that blazed within him.

His chest convulsed as organs that had been still for centuries suddenly remembered their purpose with overwhelming intensity. The sensation of his heart beginning to beat was like being struck by a thunderclap from within, each pulse sending shock waves through a body that had forgotten genuine life.

The steady thrum beneath his ribs, once borrowed time, transformed into something entirely his own. The rhythm synchronized with Caelin's as their bond settled into a pattern. "I'm alive," he whispered, pressing one hand to his chest in amazement. "Actually, completely alive."

"And beyond any future threat," she confirmed, violet fire sealing the last of the fractures Nerien's assault had carved into his essence. "I've anchored your identity so deeply in reality's foundation that not even divine intervention can threaten dissolution again."

Lucan felt the strength return to muscles that remembered their purpose with profound gratitude, sitting up with movements that spoke of weight and substance rather than mere coherence. But when he reached toward his face, fingertips seeking the golden ring that still burned around his right iris, uncertainty clouded his thoughts.

"The eye," he said, voice roughening with emotions too complex for easy naming. "It flared during the confrontation, brighter than ever. I thought your integration might heal..." he trailed off, unable to voice the hope that felt too fragile to speak aloud.

"It responds to shame," Caelin interrupted gently, replacing his fingers with her own to trace the burning mark with infinite tenderness. "You still question whether loving me was presumption rather than choice freely offered. Still wonder if mortal flesh had any right to reach for divinity."

The assessment cut through him like a blade finding every hidden wound. Through their connection, he felt her touch awakening honesty too deep for comfortable lies, forcing him to confront doubts he'd carried like poison in his veins. Yes, uncertainty remained. The brand fed on that fear, blazing brighter whenever he questioned the worth of what he'd dared to offer someone so far beyond his mortal understanding.

"Let me show you what I see," she whispered, cupping his face as light gathered around her palms. Her touch sent warmth racing through him, not just physical sensation but the promise of healing he'd never dared hope for. "Let me heal not just the effect but the wound it represents."

Power flowed from Caelin's touch into the judgment brand, transforming its meaning entirely. Lucan felt the change beginning deep within the mark itself. Where once it had burned with reminders of transgression, her divine energy rewrote its purpose from the foundation upward.

"You are not marked for arrogance," she said, her voice carrying harmonics that resonated through his bones and settled into truth. He felt her absolute conviction flooding through him, washing away centuries of self-recrimination. "You are worthy of divine love because you never demanded it as your right. Worthy because you taught immortal beings that some bonds matter more than eternal law."

Heat built behind the golden ring as her power worked, burning away shadows that had lingered too long in his soul. The golden ring flickered once, twice, then dissolved completely from his iris. Both eyes now held the same deep brown depths. Lucan blinked, stunned by the sensation of wholeness washing through him.

"Now...you are complete," she breathed, and he saw wonder bloom across her features as she studied his transformed face. Despite their completed bond, her expression held the fresh amazement of someone discovering an unexpected treasure. "Completely, finally whole."

***

Lucan marveled at the transformation rippling through him. His reflection in a nearby puddle revealed a complexion that glowed with renewed vibrancy, a rich bronze hue replacing the ghostly pallor that had clung to him for centuries. He touched his cheek, feeling warmth under his fingertips. As he shifted on his feet, he noticed how shadows danced around him, no longer pooling unnaturally like before. The eeriness that once marked him as otherworldly seemed to have vanished, leaving behind something undeniably human.

"I can feel everything," he marveled, flexing fingers that trembled not with weakness but with overwhelming sensitivity to sensations he'd forgotten existed. The stone beneath his palms registered as cool but warming from sunlight. Caelin's scent reached him like starfire mixed with violet petals. The air was a symphony of contrasts, each hour offering its own unique melody.

As Lucan inhaled deeply, he noticed how the morning air was crisp and invigorating, tinged with the fresh scent of dew-kissed grass and blooming wildflowers. It was a stark contrast to the midnight air he knew so well, which wrapped around him like a velvet cloak, rich with the earthy aroma of damp soil and the faint whisper of nocturnal blooms. Morning's breath felt alive and awakening, while midnight's embrace held secrets in its hushed tones. "How did I exist without noticing such details?"

Across the Pinnacle, Lucan noticed Jalen standing with his back diplomatically turned, though the scholar's instruments hummed with readings that clearly fascinated him despite his respect for their privacy. Jalen's shoulders held a tension that Lucan recognized, someone struggling to process experiences beyond every theory he'd studied.

"The resonance readings are completely irregular," Jalen said without turning around, his voice carefully controlled despite obvious excitement. "Your integration, it's not just personal transformation. Reality itself has adapted to accommodate a new form of divine authority."

"The cosmic order has learned flexibility," Caelin confirmed as she rose beside Lucan. The air shimmered around her like heat waves over summer stone, power contained but not diminished. She extended her hand, a violet flower blooming from her palm then dissolving into light. "Law and memory, unified through choice. Even I don't know all that will follow, but the foundation beneath us holds."

Caelin extended her hand to him, helping him stand on legs that remembered their purpose with gratitude so profound he could barely contain it. Together, they approached the Pinnacle's edge, where he looked down at the city of Elowen's Fall, spreading below them like a map of possibilities made manifest.

Lucan's eyes widened as he observed the scene before him, a blend of awe and disbelief coloring his gaze. The ancient glyphs etched into the cornerstones shimmered with a vibrant glow, each symbol flickering to life as if breathing for the first time in centuries. He could almost feel the hum of preservation magic coursing through them, a testament to the divine equilibrium restored at last.

Nearby, scaffolding that had long supported frail structures appeared less necessary; Lucan noticed how the mortar seemed to knit itself together, filling gaps with an almost sentient precision. Stones shifted subtly yet purposefully, aligning themselves into sturdy formations that promised resilience for another thousand years.

In market squares, early merchants paused to admire violets blooming from solid cobblestones, their purple petals unfurling as if acknowledging a love powerful enough to change cosmic law.

"The city remembers what it was," Lucan remarked with awe as preservation efforts shifted toward true restoration. "Our bond didn't just heal the fractured Chorus; it reminded this place that hope was possible."

"Our bond," Caelin agreed, her fingers intertwining with his as they descended passages that seemed to welcome them.

"Built through every moment you refused to let our connection break."

***

As Lucan wandered through the streets, he perceived a hidden harmony in the architecture. What once seemed chaotic now revealed intricate designs, each path spiraling toward the Pinnacle like veins converging at a heart. The buildings leaned to create acoustics that captured every whispered prayer and burst of laughter, weaving them into a sacred chorus that resonated through the air.

He noticed people emerging from shops and homes, their eyes drawn to him and his companions. His senses, sharpened by vigilance, caught every flicker of emotion on their faces. Instead of awe or trepidation, the townsfolks' expressions were calm and familiar, as if greeting old friends rather than celestial figures.

"Here," Lucan said as they reached the Archives's quarter, where preservation work continued with renewed purpose. Memory stirred in his chest, fragments of duty and honor that had waited centuries for this moment. "If divine balance is truly restored, my ceremonial armor should be accessible."

Lucan guided them through the labyrinthine corridors, his memory navigating the twists and turns that time had tried to obscure. His feet moved faster than he expected, fueled by a thrill that took him aback. They descended to the lowest Archives's levels, where dust lay thick and undisturbed. The entrance to the vault loomed ahead, its surface etched with ancient glyphs that had resisted activation for countless years. As Caelin approached, the symbols flared up in a dazzling burst of light, as if bowing to her gentle command. Lucan, watching this transformation, felt an unfamiliar tension within him unravel, like a burden he had borne for ages was finally cast aside.

Jalen stood nearby, his eyes widening with awe and a hint of trepidation. "By the stars," he murmured under his breath, his voice laced with reverence and disbelief at the spectacle before him. Instinctively, his hand reached for the worn leather-bound sketchbook tucked under his arm, eager to capture the ethereal scene unfolding in front of him.

Lucan stepped into the chamber and paused. Crystalline panels lined the walls, each bearing the name of a past guardian. He ran a fingertip over the nearest surface, feeling the cool hardness beneath his palm and the weight of those legacies pressing on him.

His gaze settled on the centerpiece: a suit of ceremonial armor displayed on a raised pedestal. The breastplate's burnished steel caught the pale light, and the leather straps hung ready at its sides. He drew in a steady breath, memories of his own vows rising unbidden.

"Do you feel that?" Caelin's voice was soft but certain as she joined him. She studied the armor's etched glyphs. "They waited for you."

Lucan nodded. He stepped forward, fingers tracing the spirals carved into the metal. Each line spoke of protection and purpose, clear, deliberate symbols, not decoration. He lifted a pauldron, noting the silver embroidery on its leather backing. A gentle warmth spread through his hand.

"I thought this was lost," he said, voice low. He slid the pauldron into place, then fastened the opposite side. The clasps clicked firmly, worn but sound.

Next came the gauntlets. He eased his hands into the supple leather and flexed the fingers against their metal reinforcements. "Still solid," he murmured, securing the last buckle. The fit was exact, as if the armor remembered him.

Stepping back, Lucan took one last look around the chamber. The nameplates glowed faintly in acknowledgment. He exhaled and squared his shoulders. "Then it's time," he said, meeting Caelin's steady gaze.

***

With that, he turned toward the exit, clad once more in the uniform that marked his purpose and his place among the guardians.

237

The third bell, Bell of Names, rang out across the city, its resonant chime weaving through the air like a gentle promise. Lucan paused, feeling the sound wash over him, a blessing wrapped in melody. He could hear the preservation crews nearby, their voices vibrant and full of hope as they shouted instructions to one another. It was a refreshing change from their usual tone of sheer determination.

Merchants called out to passersby, their stalls brimming not just with goods but with endless possibilities. The laughter of children filled the streets, each giggle and shout bouncing off ancient stones that seemed to remember how to cradle joy alongside duty. Lucan smiled at the scene unfolding around him; it was as if the city itself had awakened with renewed spirit.

"What happens now?" Jalen asked as they emerged into daylight that seemed clearer than any Lucan could recall in living memory. The scholar's expression mixed curiosity with uncertainty about his place in a changed world, and Lucan recognized the look of someone trying to find their footing when every certainty had shifted beneath them.

"Now we learn what divine law looks like when it serves love rather than opposing it," Caelin replied, power settling into patterns designed to guide rather than overwhelm. "We discover how to protect choice without constraining it, preserve memory without imprisoning it."

"And me?" Jalen shifted his satchel of instruments, the weight speaking of decisions already forming despite lingering doubt.

"My original assignment no longer exists. The Order trained me to monitor divine manifestation but never to chronicle the birth of something entirely new."

His smile held wonder and determination combined. "Perhaps it's time I learned the difference between surveillance and scholarship."

***

As they walked streets that hummed with renewed possibility, Lucan watched Caelin's integrated wisdom settle into practical understanding. He could see her thoughts working through the implications, the careful consideration of how to wield power responsibly. They wouldn't rule this city through divine mandate or impose will through unquestionable authority. Instead, they would serve as guides and protectors, helping others navigate implications of a universe that had remembered how to grow.

As Lucan turned, the morning sun spilled through the fractured dome of the Sanctum Pinnacle, casting a kaleidoscope of light that danced across its ancient stones. He marveled at how it no longer stood as a relic of forbidden acts but shimmered with the hope that some choices were worth every peril they demanded. His gaze drifted upward to where stars relinquished their hold on the sky, yielding to an expanse painted in shades of blue. The surrounding air seemed to hum with intricate melodies, weaving a tapestry that embraced both harmony and transformation.

The world had learned to make room for love that refused every boundary designed to contain it. At its heart, Lucan walked beside the soul who had chosen him across lifetimes, both of them moving toward whatever came next, anchored by choice made new with every step they shared.

# CHAPTER 16
# THE CITY REMEMBERS

Three days after heaven learned to bend, Elowen's Fall stirred awake to the sound of singing stone, a low, resonant melody that echoed through the cobblestone streets like a whispered promise.

Caelin paused in the archway of the meticulously restored Archives, her ears attuned to the subtle harmonics that now wove themselves into the city's morning symphony. The preservation glyphs, etched into the stone at every street corner, emitted a soft, unwavering glow, a stark contrast to the erratic flickering that had signaled centuries of gradual decay. The ancient mortar between the bricks sealed itself with deliberate care, each crack and crevice disappearing as if erased by an unseen hand. Nearby, scaffolding stood in readiness. Its purpose shifted from desperate reinforcement to poised assistance.

These changes weren't miraculous. There was no sudden rebirth of the city's golden age. However, they carried the promise of enduring stability, a promise that had slipped through the city's grasp since the Collapse. Buildings that had quaked with uncertainty for generations now stood with newfound poise, their foundations nestled deep into soil that remembered how to cradle and support structures meant to last through ages.

"Listen," she said to Lucan, who emerged from the Archives's depths with ancient, leather-bound texts. Dust motes swirled lazily in sunbeams that filtered through the cracked windows, each beam appearing sharper and more vibrant.

"The glyphs," he said, placing the books on a long oak table. His touch was delicate, like a curator tending to a rare exhibit. "They're singing in harmony now. Not the chaotic dissonance we've heard since the Collapse but a true melody."

Through their shared bond, she felt his awe expand outward like ripples on a pond. Memory and law, once adversaries, now wove together seamlessly, making room for growth amid stability. Each mended stone carried the intention of resilience.

"The eastern wall project shows similar improvements," Lucan continued, eyes flickering with something deeper. "Magistrate Auren sent word that the binding matrices have stabilized beyond anything in recorded history. The crews work confidently now, no longer shadowed by the specter of structural failure."

"And the people?" Caelin asked, lowering herself onto the cool stone steps. Morning light danced upon her hair, illuminating the new silver threads that had woven themselves into her locks since the integration, when Nerien's celestial essence had merged with her mortal form.

"See for yourself," Lucan replied, extending his arm toward the bustling market quarter as they stepped outside. A vibrant tapestry of voices rose into air that now carried sound with unprecedented clarity. The market hummed with conversations and the rhythmic clatter of wares, a community revitalized.

***

They walked through streets alive with a symphony of sounds and colors. The air buzzed with chatter and the rhythmic clink of tools. Once, these streets had echoed with the frantic pace of preservation crews fighting against relentless decay. Now, these same crews moved with measured precision, reflecting newfound confidence in their materials. Merchants who previously sold goods out of sheer necessity now proudly displayed wares crafted with meticulous attention to detail.

The square thrummed with energy, a hub of more than just commerce. Citizens clustered around storytellers, faces alight with rediscovered tales and techniques. An elderly weaver sat beneath a canopy of brightly colored cloth, her fingers deftly creating patterns passed down from her grandmother before the Collapse. Nearby, a young metalworker taught the art of tempering blade steel, his hands moving instinctively, as if knowledge had lain dormant in his muscles.

"Seven more recovery episodes overnight!" Jalen exclaimed, approaching with arms laden with precariously balanced scrolls. His eyes gleamed with scholarly enthusiasm, but something had changed in his demeanor, a deeper appreciation for the human stories behind his research. "And marvelously, these aren't the traumatic breaks we dreaded. The memories resurface with their full complexity intact."

Caelin looked up from a parchment she was examining. "How are people managing the transitions?"

"Quite astonishingly!" Jalen retrieved a battered leather journal from his stack. "Master Kael has unearthed the entire spectrum of pre-Collapse stone-working techniques. Taria the baker now recalls recipes that weave preservation glyphs right into the dough's rise. Even children are unconsciously singing tunes their grandparents used to hum."

A flurry of activity near the fountain drew their attention. Master Kael stood at its center, his weathered hands sketching elaborate patterns in the air. Stoneworkers and apprentices gathered around him, expressions mingling awe and anticipation.

"You see," Master Kael began, his voice resonant like a well-tuned chisel on marble, "the old ways weren't about bending stone to our will. It's about forming an alliance with it. You converse with the granite, ask what it yearns to become, and then guide it there."

A young apprentice with stone dust on her cheek attempted to copy his gesture. Master Kael stepped beside her, his gentle guidance fostering understanding that transcended mere repetition. Her eyes lit up as she nodded, absorbing the subtle skill.

As Caelin watched, a comforting warmth spread through her chest, solid and grounding, like a steady drumbeat. This was integration manifesting as it should. It was not an imposition but a harmony.

Jalen's stylus danced across his journal, capturing the exchange with quiet enthusiasm. "Curious minds are sharing information within the community, bypassing the traditional top-down approach."

"Because that's how it works," Lucan explained, scanning the crowd. "Wisdom stagnates when kept under lock and key. And knowledge? If it isn't aiding someone's growth, what purpose does it serve?"

As Caelin continued to walk through the streets, her ash gray eyes absorbed the surrounding scenes. At the periphery of her vision, celestial lights flickered like distant stars, offering gentle guidance rather than commands. She felt neither all-knowing nor all-powerful but experienced a profound clarity that enabled her to draw out hidden potential from others.

***

At the eastern preservation site, Magistrate Auren over-saw crews who moved with newfound assurance. Ancient glyphs that had once flickered with uncertainty now shone with steady, radiant light. The workers no longer wore the strained expressions of people fighting a losing battle.

The magistrate nodded respectfully. "Lady Caelin, Guardian Lucan. These binding matrices are truly extraordinary. They crystallize over time, forming structures meant to last for millennia."

"The city has an innate memory for self-preservation," Caelin replied. "We're merely providing a structure for that memory to manifest safely."

The magistrate's brow furrowed momentarily. "Our preservation protocols, our documented procedures..." Then understanding brightened his expression. "We adapt as we gain knowledge, don't we? It's our experiences that redefine our methods."

"Exactly," Lucan confirmed, scanning the construction site. "Although we can't skip certain safety measures, no matter how reliable the structures seem."

Not everyone embraced the changes wholeheartedly. Near the western quarter, they encountered a small group of Order preservationists, their faces etched with uncertainty as they examined a newly stabilized archway.

"The protocols don't account for this type of structural repair," one woman argued, clutching her preservation manual. "We have no historical precedent for these matrix configurations."

"Sometimes precedent must give way to present needs," Caelin said as they approached. "The old rules were created when decay seemed inevitable. Now we can build for permanence."

The woman hesitated, then nodded slowly. "We'll need to document these changes carefully. Establish new baselines for what's possible."

"That's precisely the approach we need," Lucan affirmed. "Not abandoning caution but expanding our understanding of what's achievable."

***

As they walked through the Archives Quarter, a group of scribe-sentinels approached, their gray robes crisp despite the restoration dust that filled the air. Caelin recognized one of them, the woman she'd often seen from her apartment window before everything changed.

"Lady Caelin," the lead scribe-sentinel said with a formal bow, her leather satchel heavy with sealed documents. "Guardian Lucan. We've been reorganizing the Archives's categories to reflect the new understanding of preservation glyphs."

"How is the transition progressing?" Caelin asked, noting how the scribe-sentinels' traditional stiff demeanor had softened.

"Better than expected," the woman replied, her fingers tracing a small memory-preservation glyph on her satchel's clasp, a gesture that would have been forbidden under the old Archives protocols. "For centuries, we preserved knowledge without truly understanding its purpose. Now the texts respond to our questions rather than simply existing in controlled isolation."

"The Archives were meant to inspire, not just maintain," Lucan observed.

The scribe-sentinel nodded, a smile transforming her once-severe features. "We've opened the Third Wing to apprentice scholars. The preservation matrices are stable enough now to withstand curious hands." She hesitated, then added, "I pass your old apartment each morning. Violets grow from the windowsill stones now."

"The city remembers," Caelin said softly.

"As do we," the scribe-sentinel replied, touching her heart in a gesture of respect before continuing on her rounds, no longer just a guardian of knowledge, but a participant in its living evolution.

***

Later that afternoon, they visited the memorial garden, where the air was fragrant with violets. Families gathered around documents, reconstructing family trees that reached into pre-Collapse times. Artisans showed age-old techniques, reviving skills that had skipped generations.

"It's like witnessing the reweaving of a grand tapestry," Jalen observed, settling onto an intricately carved wooden bench. "Individuals are recognizing how their own histories weave into the evolving narrative of our city."

"Memory's true function," Caelin agreed, noting the young scholar's evolving insight. "Not just preserving what was but laying groundwork for what could become."

***

The sound of hushed laughter disrupted the garden's tranquility. A young couple appeared from behind a flowering hedge, fingers interlaced. Caelin recognized them from the restoration crews she had worked alongside for years.

"Lady Caelin?" the woman spoke with respectful nervousness. "We've been planning to speak vows together, and with the city's transformation... Could you possibly witness our binding? Not as a divine authority giving blessing, but as someone who truly understands the cost of choosing love?"

The request resonated deeply within Caelin, intertwining her human memories of community celebrations with divine comprehension of relationships that transcended individual lives.

"I would be honored," she responded warmly. "When would this celebration occur?"

"Tomorrow evening, weather permitting," the man said with relief. "In the rooftop garden, where the city bells can echo our words across all districts. A simple affair, just family and friends gathered under the open sky."

"The most meaningful celebrations rarely require elaborate preparation," Lucan remarked, his voice carrying centuries of wisdom. "They need only willing hearts and a community ready to support whatever choice is being made."

***

As the couple departed, Caelin reflected on their transformed existence. Divine power, once distant and revered, is now intertwined with mortal joy. Celestial wisdom, once whispered only in hallowed halls, is now an openly safeguarded human celebration.

Jalen's quill moved across the parchment. "The inaugural wedding post-transformation. This will offer invaluable insights into—"

"Or," Caelin interrupted gently, "it will be meaningful because two people have declared their devotion publicly. That choice deserves celebration, regardless of scholarly implications."

Understanding settled on the young scholar's face. "You're right. I'm still learning to balance documenting everything with simply experiencing what unfolds."

"A balance worth mastering," Lucan added, his fingers intertwining with Caelin's. "Some moments are worth recording, like entries in a treasured journal. Others need to be lived fully, like the fleeting taste of summer berries. The trick is knowing when to pick up the pen and when to simply savor what's happening."

***

As the seventh bell tolled across the city, its resonant chime echoed through streets with improved acoustics, reaching farther than it had in years. They walked pathways bustling with life, where the atmosphere was not one of frantic preservation but of community renewal.

The changes weren't without challenges. In the council chambers, heated debates continued about how to adapt governance to this new reality. The Order of Preservation struggled to redefine its purpose in a world where decay no longer threatened at every turn. These tensions would require careful navigation in the days ahead, a reminder that integration didn't eliminate difficulty but transformed how they approached it.

The day had been a testament to true integration: divine power intertwined with earthly endeavors, nurturing growth instead of dictating outcomes. Wisdom gently guided individuals without removing their agency. Elowen's Fall was transforming through the collective will of its people rather than distant dictates.

Evening air carried a hint of coolness as Caelin pulled her coat tighter around her shoulders. The cityscape whispered stories of resilience; buildings once scarred by loss now stood tall as symbols of hope. Each step on weathered stones echoed with history, a rhythm of memory and aspiration intertwined.

As twilight descended over Elowen's Fall, Caelin and Lucan made their way along the cobblestone path toward their home. The cool air carried the scent of fresh bread and blooming violets, a harmony of the practical and the sublime that seemed to capture the city's transformation.

***

"Lady Caelin!" called a familiar voice.

They turned to see Merra hurrying toward them, her yellow scarf a bright splash against the deepening blue of evening. The letter carrier's satchel hung at her side, bulging with correspondence.

"Merra," Caelin greeted her with genuine warmth. "How are your routes these days?"

"That's just it!" Merra beamed, her face flushed with excitement. "The strangest thing happened this morning. I was organizing my deliveries when I suddenly remembered an old weather-warding technique my grandmother used to talk about."

Caelin exchanged a knowing glance with Lucan.

"A small glyph, drawn with rainwater on the inside of your coat," Merra continued, patting her satchel. "I tried it today, and would you believe it? The downpour completely avoided me while I made my rounds! Not a single letter dampened!"

Caelin smiled, recalling their conversation, not all that long ago, when Merra had jokingly asked about glyphs to keep the rain off her route. "I'm glad you found your weather-warder, after all."

"That's not all," Merra said, lowering her voice conspiratorially. "I've been teaching it to the other carriers. We're starting a little guild of sorts, sharing these rediscovered techniques. The Preservation Society even wants us to document them properly."

"Knowledge finding its way home," Lucan observed quietly.

Merra looked at him, then back at Caelin, her expression shifting to something more contemplative. "I never understood before, you know. Why you kept to yourself all those years. I thought you were just being standoffish, but now I see you were carrying something...extraordinary."

She reached into her satchel and pulled out a small package wrapped in brown paper. "This came for you today. Special delivery from the Archives."

As Caelin accepted the package, Merra's fingers briefly brushed against hers. The letter carrier's eyes widened slightly at the contact.

"You feel different now," she said wonderingly. "Like touching a bell that's still ringing from being struck."

"We're all changing," Caelin replied gently. "Finding older, truer versions of ourselves."

Merra nodded, her gaze moving between them. "Well, I should finish my evening route. But perhaps...perhaps you might join us someday? When we gather to share our rediscovered knowledge? Both of you would be welcome."

"We'd be honored," Lucan answered before Caelin could.

After Merra departed, Caelin unwrapped the package to find a small journal, its leather cover worn with age. Inside, in faded ink, was a collection of bread-making glyphs, preservation techniques woven into recipes.

"Perfect timing," she said, showing Lucan. "For tomorrow's celebration."

"The city remembers," he replied, taking her hand as they continued homeward. "And so do its people."

Above them, the first stars appeared in the deepening sky, their light reflecting in the glyphs that lined the streets of Elowen's Falls, a city relearning how to shine.

"We did it," Lucan said, pausing at their home's threshold. They looked back at streets where lamplight mingled with the ethereal gleam of glyphs.

"We began it," Caelin replied, her smile blending satisfaction with anticipation. "The rest will unfold as we learn to live what we've chosen to believe."

Hand in hand, they stepped over the threshold into the cozy warmth of their home. It wasn't a warmth they demanded but one they had carefully nurtured, a space that honored the love that had defied the heavens, carving out room for them to grow and thrive.

# CHAPTER 17
# THE CULTIVATED GARDEN

"The mint is staging another invasion," Caelin announced from her knees, her fingers deep in the soil among the herbs. Dirt streaked across her cheek where she had pushed her dust-colored hair aside, revealing the subtle violet threads that had appeared since her integration with Nerien. The morning sunlight glinted off these strands, weaving through her hair like memories made tangible, a physical reminder of the divine essence now permanently settled within her mortal form.

Lucan paused in his task of mending the garden gate's rusty hinges, a small smile tugging at the corners of his lips as he observed her battle against the expanding carpet of green. He had spent three years sharing mornings like these with her, learning to discern the difference between her genuine frustration and the particular tone she adopted when pretending exasperation over something she secretly found endearing.

"You could always use divine authority to contain it," he suggested, his voice light with amusement. He knew well what her response would be. Their playful banter had become a cherished ritual, comfortable as worn leather gloves and twice as treasured in the quiet rhythms of their life together.

"And miss the satisfaction of digging in the dirt? Not a chance." She settled back on her heels, her worn gloves clutching a trowel that glinted in the morning sun. The surrounding garden was a vibrant tangle of color and growth, each plant vying for its place in the sunlight. Her overalls bore the evidence of her labor, streaked with mud and grass stains, and her forehead glistened with sweat despite the crispness of the early day. "Besides, the bees adore it," she continued, nodding toward the buzzing insects flitting from flower to flower. "Who am I to deny them their happy abundance?"

Their home sprawled across the eastern hillside, where the city surrendered to the embrace of wild land, a deliberate choice to position themselves at the boundary between civilization and nature, much like their existence balanced between divine and mortal. The stone and timber construction echoed the rustic charm of the landscape, with broad windows that caught the first rays of dawn, a perfect complement to her restoration work. It was nothing grand; they had chosen practicality over ostentation, valuing room for living over space meant to impress the few visitors they entertained. The warm scent of beeswax candles lingered from breakfast, mingling with the earthy aroma of herbs drying in clusters from the kitchen rafters and the pervasive scent of healing oils wafting from Caelin's workshop.

"You have dirt in your hair," he observed with a soft chuckle, setting aside the newly oiled hinges and rising to his feet. His movements were fluid and graceful, each step a testament to the wonder he still felt at his natural ease. Even after three years, the simple act of standing without conscious effort felt like an everyday miracle, a far cry from the revenant state where each movement had required deliberate concentration.

"Occupational hazard," she said, attempting to brush away the stubborn, loose strands of hair that clung to her forehead. Her gloves, coated in rich, dark soil, only spread more dirt across her skin, leaving smudges like a child's finger painting. "Though you're one to talk," she continued, glancing at his hands, "considering whatever mysterious project has left you with permanent calluses and wood stain embedded under your fingernails."

"Speaking of which," Lucan replied, reaching into his pocket with a deliberate, almost theatrical slowness and pulling out a length of soft cloth. His fingers moved with practiced precision, suggesting he had rehearsed this moment in his mind. "I have something to show you."

Caelin's eyes lit up with the eager anticipation of someone who cherished such moments over years of shared life and love.

"Another of your secretive labors? The ones you sneak away to work on when you think I'm too lost in paperwork to notice?"

"Guilty as charged," he confessed, a playful grin spreading across his face. Moving behind her, he handled the fabric with care, unfurling it into a blindfold with a gentle shake. "But this one requires proper dramatic presentation. May I?" His voice was a mixture of excitement and tenderness, matching the soft touch of his hands as he prepared the surprise.

She tilted her head back against his broad chest, feeling the warmth radiating through his shirt, comfortable with the absolute trust that three years of daily choosing had earned between them. The familiar scent of him enveloped her senses. Rich leather mingled with the smoky aroma of forge fire, and an indescribably masculine essence that was uniquely Lucan. His heartbeat thrummed steadily and strong against her shoulder blade, a reassuring rhythm that matched the peace in her heart.

"I suppose you've been patient enough with all your mysterious labor," she said, a playful smile tugging at her lips as she closed her eyes, allowing the soft, silklike fabric to settle over them like a gentle whisper. "Though I reserve the right to terrible revenge if this turns out to be something practical like a new storage shed," she teased, imagining the surprise that awaited once the blindfold lifted.

***

*Trust her,* Lucan told himself, guiding Caelin along the winding paths, their surfaces smoothed by his diligent labor over the months. His palms were clammy despite the crisp morning air, a slight tremor betraying his nerves. *Trust that she'll understand what this means.*

His heart thudded in his chest, a rapid beat fueled by a mixture of excitement and anxiety that three years of their tranquil domestic life hadn't subdued. This wasn't a mere restoration of something old or a repair of the worn and neglected. This was the birth of something new, crafted from fragments of memory and threads of hope. A gift, he hoped, that would speak volumes but feared might be dismissed as mere sentimental folly.

"How far are we walking?" Caelin inquired, her voice carrying a blend of curiosity and anticipation as they left the familiar embrace of the house's lush gardens. Her steps were sure and steady, her trust in him so complete that the blindfold over her eyes seemed almost unnecessary. "And why do I smell something that reminds me of honey and rainfall?" she continued, a hint of a smile playing on her lips as the subtle scent of blooming wildflowers mingled with the fresh, earthy scent of damp earth and recent rain, enveloping them both.

"A little farther," he whispered, though his pulse quickened like a drumbeat in his chest as they neared the narrow opening he'd hidden behind a carefully arranged curtain of lush hedges. For three months, he'd poured his heart and soul into this secret project, tilling the earth with meticulous care, nurturing seeds under the gentle caress of sunlight, and skillfully guiding celestial flowers to unfurl their ethereal beauty upon the mortal soil.

The fragrance she had picked up on grew more potent as they drew closer to the grove's threshold. It was a symphony of scents: the sweet perfume of the wildflower meadow he had lovingly coaxed to sprawl across the land, and the earthy freshness of rainwater collected in a small spring he had artfully redirected to form a glistening natural pool. But beneath these layers lingered another aroma, one that tightened his chest with anticipation, a scent so familiar, he hoped it would stir her heart with no need for a single word.

"The path turns here," he murmured, his hand resting on her elbow to guide her through the concealed entrance. His own heartbeat thudded in his ears, each beat a testament to the vitality he still marveled at after centuries of borrowed time on this earth.

"Here," he whispered, his fingers fumbling with the knot of the blindfold, each movement betraying his nerves despite his attempt to stay calm. "Open your eyes."

As the fabric slipped away, Caelin inhaled. Her breath caught in her throat.

Spread before her was a sea of violets, stretching endlessly into the hidden grove. The flowers were a tapestry of colors, shifting from deep, velvety purples to soft lavenders as the sunlight streamed through the interlocking branches of ancient oaks above. These weren't just wildflowers scattered by chance. A meticulous hand had arranged them, each plant part of an intricate design guiding her gaze toward the grove's heart. There, a natural clearing beckoned, offering a serene spot to sit and let the silk-soft petals and their intoxicating fragrance envelop her.

"Lucan." Her voice trembled, a blend of reverence and awe, as she whispered his name. She stepped forward, her eyes widening and her hand rising to cover her mouth as recognition settled in her features. "These are the same..."

***

"The exact species from our garden in heaven," he affirmed, his gaze fixed on her face, searching for any flicker of distress at the bittersweet memory of their lost paradise. "It took months of meticulous research to unearth seeds from the oldest archives, and even longer to nurture them to life in mortal soil. But they remember you, Caelin. Watch."

As she ventured farther into the grove, each flower she passed seemed to come alive, their colors intensifying with each step she took. The petals caught the violet luminescence, passing it along in a delicate cascade, as if sharing a cherished secret under the morning sky. The flowers responded not to commands but to presence, not bending to divine will but recognizing and celebrating divine essence.

"You grew this for me," she said, her voice tinged with awe as she slowly spun around, absorbing the lush expanse of vibrant flowers and verdant foliage. Each petal and leaf whispered of the countless hours he had toiled under the sun. Sunlight danced through the trees, catching the tears that trickled down her cheeks. "All those afternoons when you vanished into the fields for hours, all those times I spotted soil beneath your fingernails and you insisted it was just from working at the forge..."

"I wanted to give you something that was ours," he replied, moving closer to her, the air around them heavy with the intensity of their shared emotions radiating from her like a palpable force. "Not something preserved from before, but something new grown from old memories. Just like us."

Her kiss, brimming with gratitude and longing deepened over the years, silenced his last words. Her fingers tightened around the fabric of his shirt as she pressed into him, tears of pure joy streaming unchecked down her face. He felt a familiar surge of wonder envelop them, as her wings unfurled, shimmering into existence, summoned by the tidal wave of her emotions.

Violet flames flickered to life at her shoulders, starting as delicate wisps that gradually solidified, fueled by the growing intensity of their shared passion. Even after years of marriage, the sight of her wings still left him breathless. They unfurled, vast and majestic, though deliberately contained to a mortal scale, a reflection of her choice to limit her divine power rather than overwhelm the natural world around them. Each feather bore intricate patterns of silver-and-gold script that seemed to pulse in harmony with her heartbeat.

"Here," she whispered against his lips, her voice a gentle caress, as she led them toward the grove's lush heart, where violets formed a plush, inviting bed. "Let me show you what your devotion creates."

***

Lucan followed her into the sea of flowers, their vigor intensifying as their bodies nestled into the soft petals, the resilient stems bending without breaking under their shared presence. The feeling was as exquisite as he remembered from their first union centuries ago, yet somehow it felt renewed and transformed.

His revenant state had once allowed him to feel only distant echoes of physical sensation, like trying to grasp the world through layers of gauze. But now, everything surged through him with overwhelming intensity. The silkiness of violet petals brushed against his skin as Caelin's deft and gentle hands undressed him, their coolness contrasting with the warmth of his flesh. The crisp morning air kissed his skin, raising goose bumps that traveled along his arms in a shiver. Her skin gleamed under his touch, catching the light with a gentle brilliance, sparking cascades of starlight that seemed to make the surrounding flowers pulse in a synchronized, ethereal dance.

"I can feel your heartbeat," she murmured in awe, pressing her palm against his chest. There, the steady rhythm thumped with a vitality that announced his complete return to life. "Strong and sure and entirely your own."

"Because you gave it back to me," he replied, enveloping her hand with his own as his fingers traced the familiar, beloved curves of her body with reverent care. His memory held each line and hollow, yet now he experienced them with the vivid depth of sensation he could finally embrace. "Every choice you made strengthened it until borrowing became owning."

Her skin felt like warm silk beneath his fingers, smooth and inviting, as if it were alive with its own electricity. Every touch seemed to send ripples of pleasure through their bond, a sensation that reverberated between them like a sweet, lingering melody. When he traced the gentle curve of her breast, she pressed into his hand, her body responding with a soft, breathy moan that made the violets surrounding them burst into vibrant life, their petals shimmering like tiny, living stars.

He watched in awe as her wings unfurled further, each translucent feather catching the dappled sunlight, creating a kaleidoscope of colors reminiscent of stained glass in an ancient cathedral. His breath caught in his throat, overwhelmed by the beauty and wonder of the moment.

"This is how it was meant to be," she murmured, her voice a soft whisper of conviction as she straddled him amid the sea of violets. Her wings spread wide with an unconscious grace that seemed as natural as breathing yet carefully contained, a testament to her mastery of the divine power that could easily overwhelm this mortal space if fully unleashed. "Not desperate clinging to broken vows but choosing each other anew every day because we want to."

Lucan watched Caelin as she deliberately descended upon him. Her warmth wrapped around him like a snug, silken embrace, igniting every nerve in his body. He inhaled sharply. Each breath carried the intoxicating blend of her scent and the heady fragrance of blossoms, every fiber of his being alive to the symphony of arousal they created together.

"Caelin," he whispered, his voice low and raw. His hands settled on her hips, tracing the sleek, firm skin under his touch as she glided along him with a grace that felt almost ethereal. Through the bond they shared, he sensed her divine essence coursing through him, a warm honey mingled with the fierce intensity of liquid fire, a power that complemented and enriched his human essence without overwhelming it. "I can feel everything," he murmured, awestruck. "Every heartbeat thudding in time with mine, every breath we draw together, every place where our skin meets..."

"Show me," she whispered, her wings unfurling gracefully, their texture as smooth as violet silk, creating a cocoon that shielded them from prying eyes. "Show me how it feels to love me."

Lucan responded by drawing her closer, their lips meeting in an embrace that tasted of sweet violets and the ethereal glow of starlight. He surged upward, a potent force that enveloped her completely, their bodies moving together in an instinctive rhythm. Each movement sent a fiery rush through him, her silken warmth gripping him with such fervor that it drew a deep, resonant groan from within. Around them, the garden seemed to come alive, each flower unfurling its petals with newfound vitality, their radiance pulsing in harmony with the beating of their hearts. It was a testament to a bond that had endured the trials of death and divine judgment, evolving into a love grounded in deliberate choice rather than frantic necessity.

The sensation of her wings wrapping around him at the moment of climax struck him with wonder that transcended physical pleasure. The divine protection enveloped Lucan like a cherished embrace, its warmth seeping into his skin and spreading throughout his body. He felt the heat of their soulmarks thrum in unison, a rhythmic pulse that resonated with his heartbeat. As the surrounding grove erupted in a gentle radiance, he was aware of how shadows caressed their intertwined forms, accentuating every line and dip of their bodies. The violets surrounding them stretched open as if in greeting, releasing a sweet aroma that wrapped around him like an intoxicating promise.

He breathed in the scent, heightening his senses and deepening his connection with his beloved.

***

"Your heartbeat," she murmured against his chest afterward, lips brushing the spot where the steady pulse proved his complete restoration. Her wings had tucked around them both like living blankets woven from captured twilight while peace settled over them like dew on morning flowers.

Lucan buried his face into the silky strands of her hair, inhaling the delicate fragrance of violets mingled with the warm scent of the woman he adored. His heart beat steadily, not with the anxious tempo of a borrowed heartbeat but with the assured pace of true ownership. Each breath he drew filled him with a profound sense of being alive, a sensation that never ceased to astonish him. "Strong enough to last lifetimes?" he murmured.

"Strong enough for however long we choose each other," she replied, a gentle correction accompanied by the soft rustle of her wings folding protectively around them. Contentment enveloped them like a serene silence in the grove that had sprung from seeds of love and memory. "Which I intend to be considerably longer than mere lifetimes, if you'll have me," she added with a playful smile.

***

As the evening sky transformed into a canvas of deep violets and glistening golds, they lay entwined amid a sea of blossoms that bloomed just for them, in a world they had constructed from deliberate choices rather than celestial decrees. Tomorrow promised new challenges and simple pleasures alike: restoration projects demanding meticulous attention and community festivities seeking their presence. The balance they'd established between divine power and mortal limitations required constant vigilance. Power easily turned to dominance if not carefully channeled through love and respect.

Yet tonight was theirs, a sacred moment for two souls who had discovered that the greatest magic lay not in defying the heavens, but in crafting something precious from its scattered remnants.

In the distance, the city's bells tolled an evening sequence, each chime resonating through the air and weaving through the labyrinth of ancient stone buildings that seemed to hum in response. The notes floated over cobblestone streets where preservation glyphs now shone with steady light, echoing through narrow alleys where citizens walked with a newfound confidence in their world's stability. Yet, in their secluded garden, nestled behind ivy-covered walls and under the dappled shade of towering oaks, the only melody that resonated was the gentle, unwavering rhythm of their hearts, beating in perfect synchrony. It was as steady and reassuring as the clusters of violets, their deep purple petals nestled in the rich, dark soil, thriving in their rightful place.

# CHAPTER 18
# THE LESSON

The soft patter of little feet on the wooden floor signaled Caelin's favorite morning ritual. At four, Eliora's attempts at stealth were endearing but mostly theoretical.

"Mama," Eliora whispered, her whisper carrying across the room like a proclamation at market...

"The glyphs in the garden are singing again."

Caelin opened her eyes, meeting a face that beautifully combined her own features with Lucan's. Eliora's dark hair caught the morning light like her father's, while her eyes held the mystery of both starlight and earth. When emotions surged through her, delicate silver threads wove through her curls, a testament to the unique blend of their legacies that was neither fully mortal nor entirely divine.

Caelin sat up, feeling the familiar subtle weight shift as her consciousness rebalanced between her human perspective and the divine awareness that resided alongside it, a negotiation that had become second nature over five years of integration with Nerien. The aroma of eggs and herbs wafted in from the kitchen, mingling with Lucan's off-key humming. Even after five years of marriage, his morning songs still brought a smile to her face.

"Is that so?" she asked Eliora. "What do they sound like today, little star?"

"Like bees but more like bells," Eliora said, settling cross-legged on the bed. Her small hands moved as she spoke, causing the surrounding air to shimmer. Not the full manifestation of divine fire Caelin could summon but something uniquely Eliora's. "Papa said you could teach them different songs if you know the right marks to trace."

"Papa's right," Caelin agreed, sweeping a silver-streaked lock from their daughter's brow. The light touch sparked a momentary flash of violet between them, a subtle reaction that occurred whenever divine essence recognized itself in another. "Want to learn how to make marks that sing?"

Eliora's eyes sparkled, lighting up the room. "Yes, please! Can I make the protect ones? Like the ones that help flowers grow?"

"We'll begin with something easier," Caelin replied, her heart swelling with pride at Eliora's urge to protect rather than control, a choice that echoed the lesson she and Lucan had learned at such cost. "But yes, marks that protect and help."

***

After breakfast, eggs and honey cakes with lavender that Lucan had perfected with hands that now moved with unconscious ease through tasks that would have required painful concentration in his revenant state, Caelin and Eliora gathered in the workshop. Sunlight poured through windows that faced east toward Elowen's Fall, highlighting shelves filled with well-used tools and artifacts from city restoration projects.

The distant outline of the Sanctum Pinnacle was visible through the eastern window, its reconstructed dome catching the morning light. The seventh bell's tower stood nearby, a daily reminder of how their personal story had become interwoven with the city's rebirth.

Caelin settled onto a cushion by the low table she had added when Eliora first showed interest in the work. Practice stones lay in neat rows, each chosen for its responsiveness to beginners. "What do you remember about glyphs from watching me work?" she asked.

"They're like letters that remember things," Eliora replied, eyes fixed on the tools with genuine curiosity rather than childish impatience. "Not just words though. They remember feelings. Like making the fountain happy about its water."

"Exactly right," Caelin said, a swell of pride in her chest. Her daughter grasped intuitively what had taken her years to understand. That glyphs were more than mere symbols, and they held emotions worth acknowledging. "Each mark carries meaning and intention. When you trace them with purpose, that purpose integrates into their function."

Lucan's voice, laced with warm amusement, floated from the workshop's doorway. "Like when Mama uses the special words that make my armor remember how to shine?"

"Daddy!" Eliora's face lit up as she turned to him. He approached with evidence of his morning labor in the wood shavings on his shirt, the current phase of transforming their eastern garden shed into a workshop space for his increasingly intricate metalwork. "We're learning the happy marks today!"

"Are we?" He slid onto another cushion, joining their circle around the practice table. His movements were fluid, like someone who had never known physical limitation, though Caelin caught the momentary flex of his left hand, a subtle acknowledgment of the joint that occasionally reminded him of his former limitations. "I'd like to learn too, if that's alright with the teacher."

"Mama's the best teacher," Eliora declared with the unwavering confidence of a four-year-old. "She knows all the marks and why they work, and she knows how to help them not be scared when they're new."

Caelin felt a warm satisfaction flood through her. This was what she had scarcely dared to hope for during those days of piecing together her memories, not cosmic authority or divine mandate, but the simple joy of sharing knowledge with someone who greeted it with curiosity and wonder.

"We'll start with a basic protection glyph," she explained, picking up a smooth slate and setting it in front of Eliora. "This glyph tells the stone to hold on to safety, to guard against any harm that hinders growth."

Caelin moved her stylus with deliberate precision, the patterns forming under her hand. As she worked, she focused on the meaning behind each stroke: the curve symbolizing resilience, the circle embodying continuity, and the small marks around the edge, inviting careful discernment.

"Protection that bends," she murmured, watching the glyph smolder with a violet hue, not the intense power she could unleash when necessary but a gentle strength that harmonized with the materials. "Like willow trees surviving storms by flexing, not falling."

"It's pretty," Eliora murmured, hesitating as her hand reached toward the glowing marks before pulling back. "Can I touch it?"

"It wants you to touch it," Caelin assured her. "Glyphs like to know who they're protecting."

As Eliora's small finger tentatively traced the pattern, the light flared briefly, then settled into a steady radiance. Caelin sensed her daughter's natural empathy intertwining with the glyph's protection, aware that this was not just a tool to wield but a partnership being formed.

"Now you try," Caelin encouraged, placing a fresh piece of slate before Eliora, along with a stylus crafted for small hands. "Remember, you're not commanding the stone to obey. You're asking it to remember something beautiful it can become."

Eliora's first attempt went awry almost immediately. Her tiny hand, still developing the fine motor control needed for such precise work, wobbled significantly. The first curve of the glyph veered off course, looking more like a jagged lightning bolt than the gentle arc it was meant to be.

"Oops," she said, her lower lip quivering slightly. "It's all wrong."

"Not wrong," Lucan corrected gently. "Just finding its way. Like when I first tried to mend your wooden horse and made its leg too short."

Eliora giggled at the memory. "He looked silly standing on three legs and a baby leg."

"And what did we do?" Lucan prompted.

"Tried again," Eliora said, reaching for a fresh slate with renewed determination.

Her second attempt showed marked improvement, though the lines remained uneven. The third slate revealed steadier curves, but when she reached the intricate center pattern, frustration clouded her face.

"My fingers won't do the small parts right," she complained, her brow furrowing in concentration.

"The small parts are tricky even for grown-up fingers," Caelin assured her. "Let's try a different approach."

Caelin guided Eliora's hand, their fingers moving together. "Feel how the stylus wants to move? That's the glyph showing you its path."

On her fourth attempt, something unexpected happened. As Eliora's confidence grew, a surge of power erupted from her fingertips, a force too vast for her small frame to contain. Her eyes widened in alarm as the energy threatened to engulf the slate. A nearby vase trembled precariously on its pedestal.

"Whoa!" she exclaimed, dropping the stylus as though it had burned her. "It got all big inside!"

Caelin moved swiftly, placing her hand over Eliora's, channeling the excess energy into a controlled flow. "That's your power, little star. It's eager to help but needs gentle guidance."

"Like when I pour my milk and it goes all over?" Eliora asked, her expression serious.

Lucan chuckled. "Exactly like that. Power needs practice, just like pouring."

With Caelin's steady guidance, Eliora tried again. This time, she approached the task with focused intention, her tongue peeking out between her teeth in concentration. The lines came more smoothly, and though the center still proved challenging, the overall shape emerged recognizably.

"Look! I'm doing it!" she exclaimed as the glyph responded, a soft glow emanating from the lines she'd carved.

"You certainly are," Caelin confirmed, noting how the light differed from her own creations. Where her glyphs typically shone with steady violet radiance, Eliora's creation pulsed with a unique blend of their family's legacies, violet threads of memory and wisdom intertwined with silver strands of balance and justice, all surrounding a golden core that unmistakably reflected Lucan's protective devotion.

"It's pretty," Eliora whispered, staring in wonder at her creation. "But it looks different from yours, Mama."

"Because it carries pieces of all of us," Caelin explained, watching the light dance across her daughter's enthralled face. "See the violet? That's like my wings. And the silver threads weaving through? That's from Uncle Nerien."

"The part of you that used to be sad but isn't anymore?" Eliora asked, her perception startling in its clarity.

"Yes, exactly," Caelin confirmed, amazed by how naturally Eliora grasped concepts that had taken her far longer to understand. "And the golden center, that's your father's heart, his protection."

"But it's not just our marks," Lucan added, leaning closer to examine the unique pattern. "You've added something entirely your own."

Indeed, woven throughout the traditional glyph structure were delicate patterns that belonged to neither Caelin nor Lucan, tiny spirals that connected the disparate elements into a harmonious whole, bringing balance where there might have been conflict.

"Can I make another one?" Eliora asked eagerly, already reaching for a fresh slate.

As the afternoon progressed, Eliora crafted five more glyphs, each showing remarkable improvement. Her last attempt, a protection mark for their garden, glowed with such vibrant intensity that it cast shadows across the workshop walls.

"What's happening?" she asked, both alarmed and delighted as the light spilled beyond the slate onto the table and floor.

Before Caelin could answer, violets began sprouting from the stone floor, their purple petals unfurling in response to Eliora's creation. The blossoms appeared first around the table's perimeter, then spread outward in a widening circle, transforming the workshop into an impromptu garden.

"The flowers like my letters!" Eliora exclaimed, clapping hands that sent tiny sparks dancing through the air like captured starfire.

"The flowers know family," Caelin explained, watching Lucan lift their daughter onto his shoulders for a better view of the botanical wonder she'd created. "They've been part of our story from the beginning."

***

"Can I put this one in my room?" Eliora asked, carefully cradling her best creation. "To keep the bad dreams away?"

"Of course," Lucan answered, his expression softening. Despite years of healing, occasional nightmares still visited them both, echoes of separations that had nearly broken them. "That's what protection glyphs do best."

As evening approached, the seventh bell, the Bell of Veil-fall, rang across the city, its resonant tones flowing through structures that carried more than just sound. Its melody reached their home on the outskirts, a reminder of the community that existed beyond their walls.

"Time for dinner and stories," Caelin announced, noting Eliora's drooping eyelids despite her protests that she wasn't tired.

"Can I make more marks tomorrow?" Eliora asked, carefully setting her practice slate on the small shelf Lucan had built for her treasures.

"As many as you like," Caelin promised, helping her gather the scattered tools. "Learning takes time and patience."

"Like the city," Eliora said thoughtfully, gazing out the window toward Elowen's Fall, where preservation glyphs glowed softly in the gathering dusk. "You said it's still learning too."

"It is," Lucan confirmed, kneeling to her level. "The city learns a little more each day, just like you do."

***

As they prepared for the evening meal, with Eliora chattering excitedly about her achievements, Caelin felt Lucan's hand find hers, their fingers intertwining with practiced ease. Their connection hummed between them, the bond they had fought across realms to preserve now strengthened by the small miracle who combined the best of them both.

Through their window, Elowen's Fall hummed with the evening's peace, bells and glyphs creating a melody of communities thriving. Their daughter would grow in a world where gods and humans worked together, where love shaped the laws, and choices remained sacred.

"What will she become?" Lucan asked quietly as they watched Eliora arranging her collection of stones in patterns only she understood. Silver threads occasionally shimmered through her dark curls when concentration intensified her connection to her divine heritage.

Caelin felt the warmth of her wings as they briefly manifested, wrapping around their family before fading back into energy. "Whatever she chooses," she said, her voice steady with the certainty that had been their hard-won victory, the freedom to decide what was worth defending.

***

Not perfect but perfectly theirs.

# ABOUT THE AUTHOR

Eira Novane writes epic fantasy romance where love is both the sword and the scar. Her stories are woven with ancient magic, fractured oaths, and soul-deep bonds that defy gods, fate, and the cruelties of time. With prose that leans lyrical and emotionally resonant, she crafts sweeping narratives where the heart is always the battlefield, and every victory comes at a cost.

Eira's heroines are fierce and haunted, her heroes unrelentingly loyal or beautifully doomed, and her worlds brim with myth, ruins, and quiet rebellion. Her work is for readers who crave slow-burn intimacy, world-shaking stakes, and the ache of a love that was never meant to survive, but might anyway.

When not writing, she's playing some story driven RPG, spending quality time with her many animals, or quietly imagining another broken kingdom that needs mending.